Wilt in Nowhere

Tom Sharpe was born in 1928 and educated at Lancing College and Pembroke College, Cambridge. He did his National Service in the marines before going to South Africa in 1951, where he did social work before teaching in Natal. He had a photographic studio in Pietermaritzburg from 1957 to 1961, when he was deported. From 1963 to 1972 he was a lecturer in History at the Cambridge College of Arts and Technology. Tom Sharpe is the author of thirteen best-selling novels. His *Porterhouse Blue* and *Blott on the Landscape* were serialised on television and *Wilt* was made into a film. In 1986 he was awarded the XXXIIIème Grand Prix de l'Humour Noir Xavier Forneret. He is married and divides his time between Cambridge, England and Northern Spain.

Wilt in Nowhere

Tom Sharpe

arrow books

Published by Arrow Books in 2005

9 10 8

First published in the United Kingdom in 2004 by Hutchinson

Arrow Books
The Random House Group Limited
20 Vauxhall Bridge Road, London SW1V 2SA

Random House Australia (Pty) Limited
20 Alfred Street, Milsons Point, Sydney,
New South Wales 2061, Australia

Random House New Zealand Limited
18 Poland Road, Glenfield
Auckland 10, New Zealand

Random House (Pty) Limited
Endulini, 5a Jubilee Road, Parktown, 2193, South Africa

The Random House Group Limited Reg. No. 954009
www.randomhouse.co.uk

A CIP catalogue record for this book is available from the British Library

Papers used by Random House are natural,
recyclable products made from wood grown in sustainable forests.
The manufacturing processes conform to the environmental regulations
of the country of origin

ISBN 0 09 947413 1

Typeset by SX Composing DTP, Rayleigh, Essex
Printed and bound in the United Kingdom by
Bookmarque Ltd, Croydon, Surrey

1

'God, what a day,' said Wilt as he and Peter Braintree sat in the garden of the Duck and Dragon with their beers and watched a lone oarsman scull down the river. It was summer and the evening sun glinted on the water. 'After that bloody Entitlement meeting I had to tell Johnson and Miss Flour they've been made redundant because of the financial cuts, and then after I was told that the Computer Department is going to do next year's time-table and I don't have to bother, the Vice-Principal sends a memo to say there's a glitch in the programme or something and I've had to do it myself.'

'You'd think the one thing a computer would be good at was sorting classes and putting them in the right rooms. All it requires is logic,' said Braintree, Head of English.

'Logic, my foot. Try using logic with Mrs Robbins who won't teach in Room 156 because Laurence Seaforth is next door in 155 and she can't make herself heard for the din his drama class makes. And Seaforth won't move because he's used 155 for ten solid years and the acoustics are just right for declaiming "To be or not to be" or Henry V's speech at Agincourt in multi-decibels. Try getting a computer to take that into account.'

'It's the human factor. I've had the same sort of trouble

with Jackson and Ian Wesley. They're supposed to grade the same exam papers and if Jackson marks a paper high, Wesley invariably says it's lousy. Human factor every time.'

'Inhuman factor in my case,' said Wilt. 'I've been dragooned into taking Ms Lashskirt's class in Gender Assertiveness because the Sociology Department refuse to have her and she has been off sick for a month. You want to try coping with fifteen mature women who are determined to assert their assertiveness and don't need to learn how to. I come out of that class a broken man. Last week I was fool enough to say women were more successful on committees than men because they never stop talking. I might just as well have stuck a stick into a hornet's nest. And when I get home Eva gives me hell. Why does everyone feel the need to be so bloody aggressive these days? Look at that.'

A motor launch had come round the bend in the river and swamped the lone oarsman's boat. He pulled in to the bank to bale it out.

'There's a speed limit on the river and that bastard was exceeding it,' said Braintree.

'There's a time limit in our house and I'm exceeding it,' said Wilt. 'Tonight we've got people coming as well. All the same if I'm going to be late I may as well have another pint to soften the blow.'

He got up and went into the pub.

'Who's coming tonight?' Braintree asked when Wilt came back with two pints.

2

'The usual. Mavis and Patrick Mottram and Elsa Ramsden with yet another acolyte who writes and recites poetry, I expect. Not that I'm going to be around. I get enough hell during the day.'

Braintree nodded.

'I had La Lashskirt and Ronnie Lann at me the other day in the Staff Room about raising student consciousness multi-sexually. I told them the students I have are far more multi-sexually conscious than I am or ever was and besides I object to this emphasis on sexuality for eleven-year-olds. Lashskirt wants to run a course on oral sex and clitoral stimulation for Nursery Nurses. I said to hell with that.'

'I can't see that going down with Mrs Routledge. She'll blow her top.'

'Blown it already. With the Principal no less at the Recruitment Meeting,' said Braintree. 'Told him she would raise the matter with the Education Authority and see how they liked it.'

'What did the Principal have to say about that?' asked Wilt.

'Said we had to keep up with modern attitudes and practices and how we needed to attract students. Numbers are all that count these days. Old Major Millfield then joined in and said sodomy was sodomy and since it was strictly forbidden in the Old Testament he couldn't see how it could possibly be described as "a modern practice". There was a right old barney.'

Wilt sipped his beer and shook his head.

3

'What beats me is why anyone should think that sort of stuff is going to attract the sort of students we need. Wait till I tell Eva. She'd go out of her mind if she thought the quads were getting lessons about clitoral stimulation and oral sex. That's one reason she sent them to the Convent.'

'I thought she did it out of religious conviction,' said Braintree. 'Didn't she have some sort of religious experience a year ago?'

'She had something. With a creature who claimed to be a New Age Pentecostalist. I prefer not to think what that something was. Religious conversion it wasn't.'

'A New Age Pentecostalist? Don't Pentecostalists speak with tongues?'

'That's not the only thing this one did with her tongue. In the shower. Yes, I know, you want to know, what were they doing in the shower together? Well, as a matter of fact this mad cow – her name was Erin Moore by the way – well, Erin said it was a necessary part of the rebirth or baptismal process, a form of total immersion so that the spirit could enter the body. I think there was some confusion about spirits and tongues. I wasn't in the house at the time, thank heaven, and Eva wouldn't tell me afterwards. Said it was too disgusting. The long and the short of it was Eva came off Pentecostalism like a shot and so did the mad cow with the tongue. Eva half killed her and the damage in the bathroom had to be seen to be believed. The shower rail came down and the shower head. Eva used it as a battleaxe. And the wall cabinet. There was glass from broken bottles everywhere and of course the shower pipe went berserk and writhed all over the place. Eva was too intent on murdering the bloody woman to think of turning the water off. She chased the creature round the house and out into the street, naked of course and bleeding. By that time the bathroom was flooded and water was stacking up above the kitchen ceiling. Naturally that came down and burst. Half a ton of water cascaded down on to the top of the fridge. I suppose it's warm and if there's one thing Tibby doesn't like it's water. Got a phobia about the stuff ever since the girls tried to give her swimming lessons in the garden pond and damned near drowned the poor beast. The consequence of the downpour from the bathroom was that she went up the wall, literally, and round it. Eva's very proud of the ornamental plates she's collected on the Welsh dresser. They weren't there by the time that cat had finished. The electric kettle went for a burton, and the Magimix machine. Both on the floor. And just to round things off the lights blew. In fact the entire electricity failed. Looked like the place had been hit by a bomb and it certainly cost a bomb to repair. As if that wasn't bad enough the insurance people wouldn't cough up because Eva refused to tell the bloke who came round what had actually happened. Said it had been an accident. He didn't believe that for a moment. Shower heads don't get ripped off by accident and the insurance company wasn't going to be ripped off either. The only good thing to come out of the ghastly business was that it got Eva off the God trot and no mistake.'

'And what happened to the tongue lady?'

'Went back into the loony bin she'd come out of. That is, when she was well enough to leave hospital. Turned out she was a card-carrying schizophrenic with religious mania. Fortunately she explained her injuries by saying she had been wrestling with an angel or a devil though she had no idea why she'd been wearing a shower cap.'

'Yes, but I still don't understand why Eva sent the quads to the Convent if she's gone off religion. The whole point about the Convent is that it's religious and Catholic at that.'

'Ah, but that's because you don't understand how her mind works. Eva goes from one extreme to another. She's not having the girls go to a state school because at the primary school they went to in Newhall the teacher had the entire class sit in cardboard boxes all morning one day – they were six at the time – because this was supposed to make them "aware". Yes I know how you feel about "awareness", it's the same as "consciousness-raising", but they had to learn what it felt like to sleep rough in a cardboard box in the street in London. That finished Eva. She told the Headmistress her daughters weren't going to end up sleeping rough and she'd sent them to school to learn to read and write and do arithmetic, not to play silly games in cardboard boxes. She made the same point at the Parent–Teacher Association meeting and wanted to know when the school was going to issue the six-year-olds with leather miniskirts and boots so they could become "aware" what it was like to be a teenage whore.

And you know what the people in Newhall are like.'

'Don't I just. Betty's mother lives over there and the house is always full of Gucci socialists with incomes up in the six figures who still think Lenin had his heart in the right place.'

'After that and the tongue lady Eva went to the other end of the spectrum. Costs a small fortune at the Convent but at least they teach them properly and believe in authority. Which reminds me, I'd better be getting back. Eva's in a nasty temper these days because I won't go hillwalking in the Lake District for the fifth year running. Says she wants a family holiday.'

He finished his beer and cycled back to Oakhurst Avenue to find Eva in a surprisingly good mood.

'Oh, Henry, isn't it wonderful. We're going to America,' she said excitedly. 'Uncle Wally has sent us free tickets. Auntie Joan's ever so pleased. She phoned to see if we'd got the tickets and they arrived this morning. Isn't it—'

'Wonderful,' said Wilt and went into the lavatory to rid himself of the beer and hide from the jubilation.

2

Eva had had a glorious day. From the moment the tickets had arrived she had been busy calculating how much Uncle Wally was worth, wondering what clothes would make the best impression in Wilma, Tennessee and how she was going to make the quads stop using foul language. The latter point was the most important. Uncle Wally was deeply religious and didn't approve of strong language. He was also a Founding Father of the Church of the Living Lord in Wilma and it wouldn't do to have Samantha saying 'Fuck' or something worse in his presence. Wouldn't do at all. Auntie Joan would be shocked too. Eva had hopes for the quads: Mr and Mrs Walter J. Immelmann had never been blessed with a family and Auntie Joan had once told Eva that Wally was thinking of making a will out in favour of the Wilt girls. Yes, it was vital for Samantha to be on her best behaviour. And of course Penelope, Josephine and Emmeline too. In fact the whole family, the only exception being Henry. Uncle Wally didn't approve of Henry.

'That husband of yours, honey, I guess he's a typical Englishman and got his good points but I have to tell you with those four lovely girls of yours you're going to need a breadwinner. And I mean a real one. Henry doesn't

strike me as being that ambitious and enterprising. Like
he takes life too easy. You got to put some spunk into
him, know what I mean? Like jack him up and get him
out there fighting. Make a financial contribution to your
wonderful family life. Seems to me he doesn't do much
of that.'

Eva had privately agreed that Henry wasn't ambitious.
She had spoken to him time and time again about getting
a better job, leaving the Tech and going into industry or
insurance where there was lots of money to be made. It
hadn't done any good. Henry was a stick-in-the-mud. So
now she placed all her hopes for the girls and her own old
age on Uncle Wally and Auntie Joan – who had met
Wally when he was a USAF pilot at Lakenheath in the
fifties and she'd been working in the PX. Eva had always
been fond of her auntie and she was particularly fond of
her now that she was married to Wally Immelmann of
Immelmann Enterprises in Wilma, Tennessee and had a
new ante-bellum mansion there as well as a lake house up
in the woods someplace whose name Eva could never
remember. So as she bustled about the house and
vacuumed and did the chores before going off to the
Community Centre to help out with the old people – it
was Thursday and Third Age lunch and a tea dance
afterwards – her mind was filled with glorious
expectations. She couldn't exactly bring herself to hope
that Uncle Wally have an infarct and die, or better still
that he crash that twin-engine plane he flew and that
Auntie Joan be with him at the time; such thoughts were

wicked and hid below the surface of Eva's kindly mind. All the same they weren't in their first youth and . . . No, she mustn't think like that. She must think of the girls' future and that was all a long way off. Besides just going to America was a great adventure and it would broaden the quads' outlook and give them an opportunity to see for themselves how in America anyone could make it big. Even Wally Immelmann, who before he'd joined the US Air Force had been a simple country boy on a small farm, had gone on to become a multimillionaire. And all because he had initiative. Eva saw Uncle Wally as a far better role model for her daughters than Wilt. Which brought her all the way back to the problem of Henry. She knew what he'd be like in Wilma, getting drunk in low bars and refusing to go to church and arguing with Wally about just about everything. There'd been that horrible evening in London when the Immelmanns had come over and taken them out to dinner at their terribly smart and fearfully expensive hotel. What was it called? The Tavern by the Park. Henry had got disgustingly drunk and Uncle Wally had said something about Limeys not being able to hold their liquor. Eva pushed the memory to the back of her mind and gave her attention to old Mr Ackroyd who said his piss bag had come undone and would she put it back for him. All you had to do was . . . No, she most certainly wouldn't. He'd caught her out before like that and she'd found herself kneeling in front of his wheelchair holding his penis while the other old people looked on with prurient interest and had laughed at her. She wasn't going to get caught out again by the dirty old man.

'I'll get Nurse Turnbull,' she told him. 'She'll put it back so it won't come out again.' And leaving the miserable Mr Ackroyd begging her not to, she went out and fetched the formidable Nurse Turnbull. After that she had trouble with Mrs Limley who wanted to know when the bus for Crowborough left.

'In a little while, dear,' Eva told her. 'You won't have to wait long now but I had to wait more than half an hour before it came yesterday.'

In half an hour, with any luck, Mrs Limley would have forgotten that she was nowhere near Crowborough and that the Community Centre was not the bus station, and she'd be quite happy again. And that after all was what Eva came to the Community Centre for, did everything for, to make people happy. In short she spent the morning doing her little bit of good for the Third Age and went home still thinking about going to America and how jealous Mavis Mottram would be when she heard about it. In the afternoon she prepared the smoked salmon sandwiches and dip for tonight's meeting of the Environmental Protection Group. And because there didn't seem enough smoked salmon she went round to the delicatessen and bought some rollmops just in case more people turned up than usual. And she put the vinho verde in the fridge to cool. But all the time her thoughts reverted to the problem of what the quads should wear on the trip to Wilma. She wanted them to look

12

respectable but on the other hand if she dressed them too smartly Auntie Joan might think . . . well, that she was spoiling them, and spending too much money or worse still, had the money to spend. Eva went through a series of permutations involving Auntie Joan being English herself, having been a barmaid and, according to Eva's mum, something else on the side which was probably why she was so generous now. Against that there was the fact that Auntie Joan's own mum had been a tight old skinflint and no better than she ought to have been herself, not when she was a girl that is, again according to Mum in one of her bad moods; though Eva had once heard Mrs Denton having an awful row with Joanie and shouting at her for giving herself to them Yanks for practically nothing. 'It's ten pounds in the back of a car and twenty-five if they want to go the whole way. You're just demeaning yourself for anything less.' Eva had been eight at the time and had made herself scarce before they knew she'd been listening. So now when it was important to play her cards right she had to be careful and not overdo things. Maybe if she didn't look smart herself Auntie Joan would feel sorry for her and think she spent all her money on the quads. Not that Eva minded what Auntie Joan had done in her teens. Not when she was so rich and respectable now and married to a multi-millionaire. Anyway the main thing was to see that the girls behaved nicely and that Henry didn't get drunk and say rude things about America not having a National Health Service.

In the lavatory Wilt was already thinking rude things. He was buggered if he was going to the States to be patronised by Uncle Wally and Auntie Joan. She'd once sent him a pair of Bermuda shorts with a tartan pattern and Wilt had refused to wear them even for the photo Eva had wanted to send back with a thank-you letter. He had to find some excuse.

'What are you doing in there?' Eva demanded through the door after ten minutes.

'What do you think I'm doing? Having a crap of course.'

'Well, open the window when you've finished. We've got visitors coming.'

Wilt opened the window and came out. He'd made up his mind.

'It sounds a great opportunity. Going to the States,' he said as he washed his hands in the kitchen sink and dried them on a cloth Eva had laid out to shake some lettuce in. Eva looked at him suspiciously. When Henry said something sounded great, it usually meant the opposite and he wasn't going to do it. This time she was going to see he did.

'It's just a pity I can't come,' he continued and looked in the fridge.

Eva, who'd been putting the lettuce in a clean, dry cloth, stopped.

'What do you mean, you can't come?'

'I've got that Canadian course to teach. You know, the one on British Culture and Tradition I did last year.'

'You said you weren't going to do it again. Not after all that trouble there was last time.'

'I know I did,' said Wilt and helped himself to the hummus with a piece of Ryvita. 'But Swinburne's wife is in hospital and he can't leave the children. So I've got to take his place. I can't get out of it.'

'You could if you really wanted to,' said Eva and vented her feelings by shaking the lettuce cloth vigorously out the back door. 'You just want an excuse, that's all. You're frightened of flying. Look how you were when we went to Marbella that time.'

'I am not frightened of flying. It was all those football hooligans getting pissed and fighting on the plane that had me worried. Anyway that's beside the point. I've agreed to take Swinburne's place. And we'll need the money the way you're bound to spend it over there.'

'You haven't been listening. Uncle Wally's paying for the trip and all our expenses and . . .'

But before they could get into a real argument the doorbell rang and Sarah Bevis arrived. She was carrying a roll of posters. Behind her a young man held a cardboard box. Wilt hurried out the back door. He'd go to an Indian restaurant for a meal.

3

Next morning Wilt was up early and he cycled down to the Tech. He had to speak to Swinburne and get him to agree to swap.

'The Canadian course has been scrapped. I thought you knew,' Swinburne told Wilt when he finally found him in the canteen at lunch-time. 'Not that I care though I could have done with the money.'

'Any particular reason?'

'Sex. Roger Manners screwed some woman from Vancouver last year.'

'What's so special about that? He's always acting like a goat. The silly ass is sex mad.'

'Chose the wrong woman,' said Swinburne. 'Got her pregnant which wasn't very wise because her husband had had a vasectomy. Came as a nasty surprise having a pregnant wife. So nasty he flew over from Vancouver and tracked Roger the Lodger down and then went to the Principal with the good news.'

'Which was?'

'That he was getting a divorce and Roger was the co-respondent. And secondly that he owned a TV station and several newspapers across Canada and that he intended to see the Tech got maximum publicity for running a course on British Culture and Tradition that included extramarital sex. Bam went the course. I'm surprised you didn't know.'

Wilt took the bad news back to Peter Braintree.

'I've got to think of something quick. I'm damned if I'm going to Wilma.'

'It sounds a nice trip to me. All expenses paid, and Americans are very hospitable. Or so I've always understood.'

Wilt shuddered.

'Hospitality is one thing but you obviously haven't met Uncle Wally and Auntie Joan. Last time they were over here we had to go to dinner with them at their hotel in London. And of course it had to be the biggest, newest and most expensive hotel with dinner served in their suite. It was unadulterated hell. First we had to have what Wally calls 'real' dry martinis. God alone knows what proof the gin was but I'd say it was liquid Semtex. I was stewed to the gills by the time lobsters came. Then the biggest steaks I've ever seen. No wine. Uncle Wally reckons wine is for pansies so we had to switch to malt whisky and Coke. I ask you, malt whisky and Coca-Cola. And all the time Auntie Joan was bleating on about how wonderful it was Eva having quads and how nice it was going to be when we all came over to Wilma. Nice? Sheer murder and I'm not going.'

'Eva isn't going to be pleased,' said Braintree.

'Maybe not but I'll think of something. Stratagems and deceptions that will make my not going seem a positive boom. We must approach the problem from the psychological angle and ask why Eva is beside herself with joy. I can answer that. Not because she's visiting the Land of the Free for the first time. Oh no. She's got a hidden agenda and that is to suck up to Uncle blasted Wally and Auntie J to such good effect that, they being childless and therefore necessarily without issue, will leave their vast fortune to our four dear daughters when they finally drop off the Dralon perch and go to the Bible Belt in the sky.'

'You really think . . .' Braintree began but Wilt raised a hand.

'Hush, I am trying to. That being Eva's intention, what will put the mockers on the diabolical scheme? Frankly, loving father that I am, I'd still have to say that having Penny, Samantha, Emmy and Josephine about the house for two months ought to do the trick quite nicely. By the time they leave even Auntie Joan, who oozes senti-mentality and drools on about how cute things are, will be dying to be rid of them and Wally will celebrate their departure by throwing the biggest party Wilma's seen for years. The only snag is that I would have to be there sharing the inferno and getting the blame for their appalling behaviour. No, I shall have to think of some-thing in the way of a pre-emptive strike. I shall go away and meditate.'

He did so through an hour of Gender Assertiveness for Mature Women none of whom had anything to learn about asserting themselves. In fact they asserted them-selves so thoroughly that all he had to do was to get them going. After that he could sit back and nod and agree to everything they had to say. He had learnt the trick from Eva who was always pointing out how inadequate he was as a husband, a father and a sexual partner. Wilt had long since given up disputing his failings and now let the tide of her disapproval roll over him without really noticing it. He did the same with the Mature Women but first he had to provoke them. He did this now by pointing out that there could be no such thing as male menopause because men didn't menstruate. The resulting storm of disagreement occupied the class very happily for the rest of the hour while Wilt wondered why it was so easy to provoke people who had fixed ideas and also why, having got them going, they adamantly refused to listen to any counter-arguments. It had been the same with his old classes of Gasfitters and Printers. Then it had only been necessary to say he thought capital punishment was wrong or that there was a perfectly sound case for thinking homosexuals were born that way and all hell would break loose. Wilt considered Wally Immelmann's most violent prejudice and realised it was socialism. He particularly loathed trades unions and equated them with communists, devil worshippers and the Evil Axis. Wilt had once admitted he'd voted for the Labour Party and belonged to a trades union. The explosion that had followed suggested Uncle Wally was about to die of apoplexy. Remembering the occasion, Wilt realised he had found the solution to his problem.

When the class finished and the mature women

dispersed to assert themselves somewhere else, Wilt went across to the library and took out six books.

'And where do you think you are going with those?' Eva demanded when he got home and put them on the kitchen table and she spotted their titles.

'I've got to give a course on Marxist ideology and revolutionary theory in the Third World next term. Don't ask me why but I do. And since I don't know the first thing about revolutionary theory or Marxism and I'm not even sure there is a second world let alone a third, I have to bone up on it. I'm taking them to Wilma.'

Eva was gaping at the title of another large volume which read *Castro's Struggle Against American Imperialism*.

'Are you insane? You can't take that to Wilma,' she gasped. 'Wally would kill you. You know what he feels about Castro.'

'I daresay he doesn't like him very much . . .'

'Henry Wilt, you know perfectly well . . . you know . . . you know he was involved with whatever that attempt to invade Cuba was called.'

'The Bay of Pigs,' said Wilt and considered saying how appropriate it was for Wally Immelmann but Eva had found another book.

'*Gaddafi. The Libyan Liberator.* I don't believe it.'

'Nor do I as a matter of fact,' said Wilt. 'But you know what Mayfield's like. He's always inventing new courses and we've all got to—'

'I don't care what you've got to do,' Eva said furiously. 'You are not going to Wilma with those dreadful books.'

'You think I want to?' said Wilt ambiguously and picked up another. 'This one is about how President Kennedy wanted to use the atom bomb on Cuba. It's really rather interesting.'

There was no need to go on but Wilt did.

'Well, if you want me to lose my job, I'll leave them behind. They've already made five Senior Lecturers redundant this year and I know I'm on the short list. And with the pension I'd get we wouldn't be able to keep the girls at the Convent. We've got to think about their education and their future and there's no point my taking the risk of getting the sack simply because Uncle Wally doesn't like my reading about Marxism in Wilma.'

'In that case you are not coming,' said Eva, now thoroughly convinced. 'I'll tell them you've had to stay here and teach during the holidays to pay for the girls to go to school.' She stopped, struck by a sudden thought. 'That course for the Canadians. You said last night you couldn't come because you had to stand in for Swinburne.'

'Cancelled,' said Wilt hurriedly. 'No problem there. Not enough students.'

4

Next day while Eva was busy in Ipford trying to decide what new clothes to buy for the quads Wilt made his own preparations. He knew now what he was going to do: go on a walking tour. He had found a rain cape in the form of an old army groundsheet, a suitably shabby rucksack and a water bottle from the Army & Navy stores, and had even considered buying a pair of khaki shorts that came down over his knees only to decide that his legs weren't the sort to expose to the world and he didn't want to go round the West Country looking like a superannuated Boy Scout. Instead he chose blue jeans and some thick socks to go with the walking boots Eva had bought for their family holiday in the Lake District. Wilt wasn't sure about the walking boots. They were purpose-built for fell walking and he had no intention of going anywhere near anything resembling a fell. Tramping was all very well for them that liked that sort of thing but Wilt intended sauntering and not doing anything too strenuous. In fact it had occurred to him that it might be a good idea to find a canal and walk along the tow-path. Canals had to stick to the flat and when they came to anything resembling a hill they very sensibly made use of locks to get over them. On the other hand he couldn't find any canals in the part of the world he had in mind to walk across. Rivers were his best bet. On the whole they took even easier ways than canals and there were bound to be footpaths beside them. And if there weren't, he would take to fields provided there weren't any bulls in them. Not that he knew anything about bulls except that they were dangerous.

There were other contingencies he had to take into account, like what would happen if he couldn't find anywhere to sleep at night. He bought a sleeping-bag and took the lot back to his office and crammed it into a cupboard before locking it. He didn't want Eva bursting in unexpectedly (she did this every now and then ostensibly to collect something from him like the car keys) and finding out what he really planned to do while she was away.

But Eva had her own problems to concentrate on. She was particularly worried about Samantha who didn't want to go to America because the cousin of a friend at school had been to Miami and said she'd seen a man shot in the street there.

'They've all got guns and the murder rate is terrible,' she told Eva. 'It's a very violent society.'

'I'm sure it's not like that in Wilma. And besides, Uncle Wally is a very influential man and no one would dare do anything to make him angry,' Eva told her.

Samantha was not convinced.

'Dad said he's a bombastic old bugger who thinks America rules the world . . .'

'Never mind what your father says. And don't use words like that in Wilma.'

'What? Bombastic? Dad says that's the operative word. Americans drop bombs in Afghanistan from thirty thousand feet and kill thousands of women and children.'

'And miss the real targets too,' said Emmeline.

'You know perfectly well what word,' Eva snapped before the quads could really get going. She wasn't going to be drawn into using 'bugger' herself either.

Josephine didn't help.

'All bugger means is anal intercourse and—'

'Shut your mouth. And don't ever let me hear you using language like that in front of . . . well, anywhere. It's disgusting.'

'I can't see why. It's legal and gays do it all the time because they don't have . . .'

But Eva was no longer listening. She was facing another problem.

Emmeline had just come downstairs with her pet rat. It was a long silver-haired tame rat she'd bought at a pet shop and had named Freddy and now she wanted to take it to Wilma to show Auntie Joanie.

'Well, you can't,' Eva told her. 'That's out of the question. You know she has a horror of rats and mice.'

'But he's ever so friendly and he'd help her get over her phobia.'

Eva doubted it. Emmeline had trained it to make itself comfortable under her sweater and move about. She frequently did this when people came to tea and the effect on visitors was one of horror. Mrs Planton had actually fainted at the sight of what appeared to be a pubescent breast moving across Emmy's chest.

'In any case it's illegal to take animals out of the country and bring them back again. It might have rabies. No, it's not going and that's my final word.'

Emmeline took Freddy up to her room and tried to think which of her friends would look after it.

All in all it was a harrowing evening and Eva was not in a good mood when Wilt came home looking rather pleased with himself. Eva always had the feeling that when he looked like that he was up to something.

'I suppose you've been drinking again,' she said to put him on the defensive.

'As a matter of pure fact I haven't touched a beer all day. I have put my past excesses behind me.'

'Well, I wish you had put a lot of your filthy language behind you too instead of teaching the girls to talk like . . . like . . . well, to use filthy language.'

'"Troopers" is the word you were looking for,' said Wilt.

'Troopers? What do you mean "troopers"? If that is another filthy word I—'

'It is an expression. Talking like troopers means—'

'I don't want to know. It's bad enough having Josephine talking about buggery and anal intercourse without you coming home and encouraging them.'

'I'm not encouraging them to talk about buggery. I don't have to. They pick up far worse expressions at the

Convent. Anyway, I'm not going to argue. I'm going to have a bath and think pure thoughts and then after supper I'm going to see what's on TV.'

He stumped upstairs before Eva could get in a crack about the sort of thoughts he'd be having in the bath. In the event the bathroom was occupied by Emmeline. Wilt went downstairs and sat in the living room looking at the book on revolutionary theory and wondering how anyone in his right mind could still think bloody revolutions were a good thing. By the time Emmeline had finished with the bathroom it was too late for him to have his bath. Instead he washed and went down to supper where Eva was finding it impossible to persuade the quads to accept the clothes she had chosen for them to impress Auntie Joan with.

'I'm not going to wear a silly dress that makes me look like something out of an old cowboy movie,' Penelope said. 'Not for anyone.'

'But it's gingham and you'll all look so nice . . .'

'We won't. We'll all look ridiculous. Why can't we go in our own clothes?'

'But you want to make a good impression, and old jeans and bovver boots . . .'

Wilt left them still arguing and took himself off to the spare bedroom which he used as his study and looked at an Ordnance Survey map of the West Country and the route he would follow on his tour. Brampton Abbotts, Kings Caple, Hoarwithy, Little Birch and up to Holme Lacy by way of Dewchurch. And beyond that over the

Dinedor Hills to Hereford and the great cathedral there with the Mappa Mundi – the map of the known world when the world was young – and then on again following the River Wye through Sugwas Pool, Bridge Sollers, Mansell Gamage to Moccas and Bredwardine and finally to Hay-on-Wye and the little town of bookshops. He thought he would stay there for two or three days depending on the weather and the books he bought. After that he would head north again by way of Upper Hergest and Lower, which seemed to be above it in the map. It was an old map with a cloth back to it and it was difficult to read the names where it had been folded. It didn't show the motorways or anything built after the War but that too suited him perfectly. He didn't want the new England, he wanted old England and with names like those on the map he was bound to find it. By the time he went to bed the dispute downstairs had burnt itself out. Eva had given way on the gingham dresses and the quads had agreed not to go in their oldest and most patched jeans. Bovver boots were out too.

5

For the next fortnight Wilt kept out of the house as much as possible and occupied himself with finishing next year's timetable while Eva bustled about trying to think of essential things she might have forgotten to tell Henry to do while she was away.

'Now don't forget to give Tibby her dried food at night. She has her main tin of Cattomeat in the morning. Oh, and there's her vitamin supplement. You crush that up in a saucer and put some cream from the top of the milk on it and stir . . .'

'Yes,' said Wilt, who had no intention of feeding the cat. Tibby was going into the cattery on Roltay Road as soon as Eva and the girls were on their way to Wilma.

He solved another problem too.

He would take cash and use his Building Society savings. They had always been reserved for personal emergencies and he'd never told Eva of their existence.

He made another decision. He wasn't going to take a map. Wilt wanted to see things with a fresh eye and make his own discoveries. He would go wherever the countryside took his fancy without any idea where he was and without consulting any map. He would simply go over to the West and catch the first bus he could find and get out when he saw something that interested him. Chance would determine his holiday.

6

A week later, having driven Eva and the girls to Heathrow and seen them disappear through the Departures Gate, Wilt came back to Oakhurst Avenue and took Tibby to the Bideawhile cats' home in Oldsham secure in the knowledge that since he had paid cash and hadn't used the usual cattery Eva always went to she was unlikely to find out. Having dealt with that problem Wilt had supper and went to bed. Next morning he was up early and out of the house by seven. He walked down to the railway station to catch a train to Birmingham. From there he would travel by bus. His escape from Ipford and the Tech had begun. That evening would find him comfortably installed in a pub with a log fire and with a good meal inside him and a pint of beer or better still real ale in front of him.

Eva wasn't having quite the wonderful time she had expected. The flight had been delayed for over an hour. The plane had reached the end of the runway at Heathrow and was preparing for take-off when the Captain announced that a passenger in first class had been taken ill and was too sick to make the journey, and they were therefore having to return to the terminal to have him carried off. As a result they lost their turn in the take-off line and worse still, because they weren't allowed to fly with the baggage of an absent passenger, his bags had to be found and removed too. Finding the sick man's luggage meant taking all the bags out of the hold and sorting through them one by one. By that time they were well behind schedule and Eva, who had never flown in such a big plane before, was beginning to become genuinely alarmed. Of course she couldn't show it in front of the girls who were thoroughly enjoying themselves pressing buttons so that the seats tilted backwards and trying on the earphones and letting down the tables from the seat in front and generally occupying themselves to the discomfort of other passengers.

Then Penelope had insisted in a loud voice that she had to go to the loo and Eva had had to squeeze past the man at the end of the row to go with her. When they got back and Eva had squeezed back to her seat, Josephine said she had to go too. Eva took her and Emmeline and Samantha just to be on the safe side. By this time – and they had taken their time trying out various buttons and the toilet water – Eva needed to go herself and just at that moment it was announced that passengers had to return to their seats for take-off. Eva once more made the difficult passage past the man at the end of the row who said something in a foreign language which she didn't understand but which she suspected wasn't very nice. Then when they had reached cruising height and she could go again and in something of a hurry too, what he had to say didn't require any knowledge of a foreign language to tell her that it wasn't nice at all. Eva got her own back by treading on his foot when she resumed her seat. This time there could be no mistaking his feelings. 'Fuck,' he said. 'Mind where you're treading, lady. I ain't no doormat.'

Eva pressed the button for the stewardess and reported the matter.

'This man – I won't call him a gentleman – said . . .' She paused and remembered the quads. 'Well, he used a rude word.'

'He said "Fuck",' Josephine explained.

'He said "Fuck you",' Penelope added.

The stewardess looked from Eva to the girls and knew it was going to be a bad trip.

'Yes, well, some men do,' she said pacifically.

'No, they don't,' said Samantha. 'Not impotent ones. They can't.'

'Shut your mouth,' Eva snapped and tried to smile apologetically at the stewardess who wasn't smiling at all.

'It's true,' Emmeline joined in from across the aisle. 'They can't get erections.'

'Emmeline, if I hear another word out of you,' Eva bawled. 'I'll . . .' She was getting to her feet when the man beside her got there first.

'Listen, lady, I don't give a goddam fuck what she said. You ain't corn-crushing my feet again.'

Eva looked triumphantly at the stewardess.

'There you are, what did I tell you?'

33

But the man was also appealing to the stewardess.

'You got another seat? I'm not spending seven hours sitting next to this hippopotamus, I'm telling you I'm not.'

It was a thoroughly unpleasant scene and when it had been cooled down and the man had been found another seat as far away from Eva and the quads as possible, the stewardess went back to the galley.

'Row 31 is trouble. Keep your eyes open. Four girls and a mother who is built like a power lifter. Sperm bank her with Tyson and there's no one would go a single round with the baby.'

The steward looked down the rows.

'Thirty-one is suspect,' he said.

'Don't I know it.'

But the steward was looking at the man in the window seat. So were two men in grey suits five seats behind him.

That was the beginning of the flight. It didn't get much better. Samantha spilt her Coke, all of it, on the trousers of the man by the window, who said, 'Forget it, these things happen,' though he didn't say it very nicely and then went off to the toilet. On the way there he noticed something that caused him to spend a far longer time locked inside than was needed for cleaning his trousers or even relieving himself. Still in the end he came out looking fairly calm and went back to his seat. But before sitting down he opened the hand-luggage compartment above and found a book. It took him some moments to get it out but in the end he succeeded and to avoid having a Coca-Cola spilt on his trousers again he offered to sit in the aisle seat.

'The little lady can have the window,' he said with a sweet smile. 'I got more room for my legs here.'

Eva said that was real kind of him. (She was beginning to adjust her language to American and 'real' was just as good as 'really'.) She was also beginning to distinguish between nice Americans who didn't complain when one of the quads spilt things on them and were polite and called them little ladies, and the other sort who said 'Fuck' and called her a hippopotamus just because she stepped on their toes. After that the flight continued pretty harmoniously. There was a movie which kept the girls interested and Eva concentrated on what she was going to say to Uncle Wally and Auntie Joan about how kind it had been of them to invite them over and pay for the tickets especially as there was no way she could have come the quads' education cost so much and clothing them etc. In fact she dozed for a while and it was only when the stewardesses came round with the trolley again and they had something more to eat that she woke up and took particular care to see that there was no more spilling on people's trousers.

In fact she got talking with the nice man in the aisle seat who asked if this was her first trip to the USA and where she was going, and who was real interested to learn everything about her and the girls and even went so far as to write their names down and said if they ever came down Florida way this was his address. Eva really liked him; he was so charming. And she told him all about how Wally Immelmann was head of Immelmann Enterprises in Wilma, Tennessee, and had a lakeside house up in the Smokies and how her Auntie Joan had married him when he was at the airbase and an Air Force pilot flying out of Lakenheath, and the man said he was Sol Campito and he worked with a Miami-based finance corporation and sure he'd heard of Immelmann Enterprises, like everyone had it was so important. An hour later he took another 'hygiene break' which was a new term for Eva and meant going to the toilet again. This time he didn't take so long and when he came back he put his book away in the luggage compartment and said he was going to get some shut-eye because he had to catch the shuttle flight down to Miami and it was a long trip from where he'd come, like Munich, Germany, where he'd had some business. And so the flight wore on and nothing untoward occurred except that Penelope kept asking when they were going to get to Atlanta because she was bored and Sammy wouldn't let her have the window seat so she could look out at the clouds. Behind them the two men in grey suits watched the man who had given up his window seat for Samantha. One of them took himself off to the toilet and was in there for five minutes. He was followed half an hour later by the second suit who stayed even longer. When he came back he shrugged as he sat down. Finally by the time Eva was getting really tired the Jumbo was slowly dropping down towards the land and the countryside seemed to be coming up to them and the undercarriage was locked down and the flaps were up and they were down with only a slight thump and lurch and into reverse thrust.

'The land of the free,' said the man with a smile when they were at the terminal and could collect their bags from the overhead lockers; he was on his feet helping to get Eva's and the quads' stuff for them. And then he very politely stood in the aisle in the way of the other passengers to let them file out first. In fact he let a number of other passengers go in front of him and only then moved himself. By the time they had collected their hold luggage from the carousel he was nowhere to be seen. He sat in the toilet writing the address and the names Eva had given him before he came out. Twenty minutes later Eva and the quads passed through Immigration and Customs where they were held up for some time and a German Shepherd took an interest in Emmeline's hand luggage. Two men studied the family for two minutes and then they were through and there was Uncle Wally and Auntie Joan and there was all the hugging and kissing imaginable. It was wonderful.

It wasn't quite so wonderful in a little room back in Customs for the man who'd called himself Sol Campito. The things from his travel bags were spread out on the floor and he was standing naked in another booth with a man with plastic gloves on his hand telling him to get his legs open.

'Wasting time,' said one of the men in the room. 'Give him the castor oil and blow the fucking condoms out quicker, eh Joe? You crazy enough to have swallowed the stuff?'

'Shit,' said Campito. 'I don't do no drugs. You got the wrong guy.'

Four men in an office next door watched him through a darkened observation window.

'So he's clean. Met the contact in Munich and left with the stuff. Now he's clean. Then it's got to be the fat Brit with the kids. How did you assess her?'

'Dumb. Dumb as hell.'

'Nervous?'

'Not at all. Excited yes but nervous no way.'

The second man nodded.

'To Wilma, Tennessee.'

'And we know where she's going. So we keep her under observation. The tightest possible. OK?'

'Yes, sir.'

'Just make sure you keep under cover. The stuff that bastard's said to have picked up from Poland is lethal. The good thing is we know from his notebook where that Wilt woman is heading with that foursome. Get there fast. This surveillance has top priority. I want to know all there is to know about this Immelmann guy.'

7

Wilt's day had begun badly and got steadily worse. All his
hopes and expectations of the previous evening had
proved terribly wrong. Instead of the homely pub with a
log fire, and a good meal and several pints of beer or
better still real ale inside him, and a warm bed waiting for
him, he found himself trudging along a country lane with
dark clouds closing in from the West. In many respects it
had been a disastrous day. He had walked the mile and a
half to the station with his knapsack on his back only to
find that there were no trains to Birmingham because of
work on the line. Wilt had had to take a bus. It was a
comfortable enough bus – or would have been if it hadn't
been half filled with hyperactive schoolchildren under
the charge of a teacher who did his level best to ignore
them. The rest of the passengers were Senior, and in
Wilt's opinion Senile, Citizens, out on a day-trip to enjoy
themselves, a process that seemed to consist of complaining loudly about the behaviour of the hyperactive kids
and insisting on stopping at every service station on the
motorway to relieve themselves. In between service
stations they sang songs Wilt had seldom heard before
and never wanted to hear again. And when finally they
reached Birmingham and he bought a ticket for Hereford

he had difficulty finding the bus. In the end he did. It was a very old double-decker bus with a faded 'Hereford' sign on the front. Wilt thanked God there were no other passengers in it. He'd had enough of small boys with sticky fingers climbing across his lap to look out the window and of old age pensioners singing, or at any rate caterwauling, 'Ganging along the Scotswood Road to see the Blaydon Races' and 'We're going to hang out the washing on the Siegfried Line'. Wilt climbed wearily into the back and lay down across the seat and fell asleep. When the bus left he woke up and was surprised to find he was still the only passenger. He went back to sleep again. He had only had two sandwiches and a bottle of beer all day and he was hungry. Still, when the bus got to Hereford he'd find a café and have a good meal and look for a bed and breakfast and in the morning set out on his walking tour. The bus didn't get to Hereford. Instead it stopped outside a shabby bungalow on what was clearly a distinctly B road and the driver got out. Wilt waited ten minutes for him to return and then got out himself and was about to knock on the door when it opened and a large angry man looked out.

'What do you want?' he demanded. In the bungalow a Staffordshire bull terrier growled menacingly.

'Well, as a matter of fact I want to go to Hereford,' said Wilt, keeping a wary eye on the dog.

'So what are you doing here? This isn't bloody Hereford.'

Wilt produced his ticket.

'I paid my fare for Hereford in Birmingham and that bus—'

'Isn't going nowhere near Hereford. It's going to the fucking knacker's yard if I can't flog the fucker first.'

'But it says "Hereford" on the front.'

'My, oh, my,' said the man sarcastically. 'You could have fooled me. You sure it don't say "New York"? Go and take a dekko and don't come back and tell me. Just bugger off. You come back and I'll set the dog on you.'

He went back into the bungalow and slammed the door. Wilt retreated and looked at the sign on the bus. It was blank. Wilt stared up and down the road and decided to go to the left. It was then he noticed the scrapyard behind the house. It was full of old rusting cars and lorries. Wilt walked on. There was bound to be a village somewhere down the road and where there was a village there was bound to be a pub. And beer. But after an hour in which he passed nothing more accommodating than another awful bungalow with a 'For Sale' sign outside it, he took his knapsack off and sat down on the grass verge opposite and considered his situation. The bungalow with its boarded windows and overgrown garden wasn't a pleasing prospect. Lugging his knapsack Wilt moved a couple of hundred yards down the lane and sat down again and wished he'd bought some more sandwiches. But the evening sun shone down and the sky to the east was clear so things weren't all that bad. In fact in many ways this was exactly what he had set out to experience. He had no idea where he was and no wish to know. Right from the start he had intended to erase the map of England he carried in his head. Not that he ever could; he had memorised it since his first geography lessons and over the years that internal map had been enlarged as much by his reading as by the places he'd visited. Hardy was Dorset or Wessex, and Bovington was Egdon Heath in *The Return of the Native* as well as where Lawrence of Arabia had been killed on his motorcycle; *Bleak House* was Lincolnshire; Arnold Bennett's *Five Towns* were the Potteries in Staffordshire; even Sir Walter Scott had contributed to Wilt's literary cartography with *Woodstock* and *Ivanhoe*. Graham Greene too. Wilt's Brighton had been defined for ever by Pinkie and the woman waiting on the pier. But if he couldn't erase that map he could at any rate do his best to ignore it by not having a clue where he was, by avoiding large towns and even by disregarding place names that might prevent him from finding the England he was looking for. It was a romantic, nostalgic England. He knew that but he was indulging his romantic streak. He wanted to look at old houses, at rivers and streams, at old trees and ancient woods. The houses could be small, mere cottages or large houses standing in parkland, once great mansions but now in all probability divided up into apartments or turned into nursing homes or schools. None of that mattered to Wilt. He just wanted to wash Oakhurst Avenue, the Tech and the meaninglessness of his own routine out of his system and see England with new eyes, eyes unsullied by the experience of so many years as a teacher.

Feeling more cheerful he got to his feet and set off again; he passed a farm and came to a T-junction where he turned left towards a bridge over a river. Beyond it there was the village he had been looking for. A village with a pub. Wilt hurried on only to discover that the pub was shut for refurbishment and that there were no cafés or B & B guest-houses in the place. There was a shop but that too was shut. Wilt trudged on and finally found what he was looking for, an old woman who told him that, while she didn't take lodgers in the normal way, he could stay the night in her spare bedroom and just hoped he didn't snore. And so after a supper of eggs and bacon and the down payment of £15 he went to bed in an old brass bedstead with a lumpy mattress and slept like a log.

At 7 the old woman woke him with a cup of tea and told him where the bathroom was. Wilt drank the tea and studied the tintypes on the wall, one of General Buller in the Boer War with troops crossing the river. The bathroom looked as if it had been around during the Boer War too but he had a shave and a wash and then another apparently inevitable helping of bacon and eggs for breakfast, and thanked the old woman and set off down the road.

'You'll have to get to Raughton before you find a hostel,' the old woman, Mrs Bishop, told him. 'It's five miles down thataway.'

Wilt thanked her and went down thataway until he came to a path that led uphill into some woods and turned off along it. He tried to forget the name Raughton, perhaps it was Rorton, and whatever it was he no longer cared. He was in the English countryside, old England, the England he had come to discover for himself. For half a mile he climbed up the hill and came out on to a stunning view. Below him a patchwork of meadows and beyond them a river. He went down and crossed the empty fields and presently was standing looking at a river that flowed, as it must have done for thousands of years, down the valley, in the process creating the flat empty fields he had just crossed. This was what he had come to find. He took off his knapsack and sat on the bank and watched the water drifting by with the occasional ripple that suggested a fish or an undercurrent, some hidden obstacle or pile of rubbish that was sliding past under the surface. Above him the sky was a cloudless blue. Life was marvellous. He was doing what he had come to do. Or so he thought. As ever in Wilt's life he was moving towards his Nemesis.

It lay in the vengeful mind of a justifiably embittered old woman in Meldrum Slocum. All her working life, ever since she had entered the service of General and Mrs Battleby forty-five years before, Martha Meadows had been the cleaner, the cook, the housekeeper, the every help the General and his wife depended on at Meldrum Manor. She had been devoted to the old couple and the Manor had been the centre of her life but the General and his wife had been killed five years before in an accident with a drunken lorry driver; the estate had been taken over by their nephew Bob Battleby and everything had changed. From being what the old General had called 'our faithful retainer, Martha', a title of which she had been exceedingly proud, she had found herself being called that 'bloody woman'. In spite of it she had stayed on. Bob Battleby was a drunk, and a nasty drunk at that, but she had her husband to think of. He'd been the gardener at the Manor but a bout of pneumonia followed by arthritis had forced him to leave his job. Martha had to work and there was nowhere else in Meldrum she could find employment. Besides, she had hopes that Battleby would drink himself to death before too long. Instead he began an affair with Ruth Rottecombe, the wife of the local MP and Shadow Minister for Social Enhancement. It was largely thanks to her that Martha had been replaced by a Filipino maid who was less disapproving of what they called their little games. Martha Meadows had kept her thoughts to herself but one morning Battleby, after a particularly drunken night, had lost his temper and had thrown her things – the clothes she came in before changing into her working ones – into the muddy yard outside the kitchen; he had called her a fucking old bitch and better off dead at that. Mrs Meadows had walked home seething with rage, and determined on getting her own back. Day after day she had sat at home beside her sick husband – who'd recently had a stroke and couldn't talk – grimly determined to get her revenge. She had to be very, very careful. The Battlebys were a rich and influential family in the county and she had often thought of appealing to them, but for the most part they were of a different generation to the General's nephew and seldom came to the Manor. No, she would have to act on her own. Two empty years passed before she thought of her own husband's nephew, Bert Addle. Bert had always been a bit of a tearaway but she'd always had a soft spot for him, had lent him money when he was in trouble and had never asked for it back. Been like a mother to him, she had. Yes, Bert would help, especially now he'd just lost his job at the shipyard at Barrow-in-Furness. What she had in mind would certainly give him something to do.

'He called you that?' Bert said when she told him. 'Why, I'll kill the bastard. Calling my auntie a thing like that when you've been with the family all those years. By God, I will.'

But Martha shook her head.

'You'll do no such thing. I'm not having you go to prison. I've got a better idea.'

Bert looked at her questioningly.

'Like what?'

'Disgrace him in public, so he can't show his face round here no more, him and that hussy of his. That's what I want.'

'How you going to do that?' Bert asked. He'd never seen Martha so furious.

'Him and that Rottecombe bitch get up to some strange things, I can tell you,' she said darkly.

'What sort of things?'

'Sex,' said Mrs Meadows. 'Unnatural sex. Like him being tied up and . . . Well, Bert, I don't like to say. But what I do say is I've seen the things they use. Whips and hoods and handcuffs. He keeps them locked away along of the magazines. Pornography and pictures of little boys and worse. Horrible.'

'Little boys? He could go to prison for that.'

'Best place for him.'

'But how come you've seen them if they're locked away?'

'Cos he was so drunk one morning he was dead to the world in the old General's dressing room and the cupboard was open and the key still in the lock. And I know where he keeps his keys, like the spare ones. He don't know I do but I found them. On a beam over the old tractor in the barn he don't ever use and can't cos it's broken. Shoves them up there where no one would think of looking. I seen him from the kitchen window. Keys of the back and front doors, key of his study and his Range Rover and the key of that cupboard with all that filth in it. Right, now here's what I want you to do. That is if you're prepared to, like.'

'I'd do anything for you, Aunt Martha. You knows that.'

By the time he left Bert knew exactly what he had to do.

'And don't you come in your car,' Martha told him. 'I don't want you getting into trouble. You hire one or something. I'll give you the money.'

Bert shook his head.

'Don't need to. I've got enough and I know where I can get something to use, never you worry,' he said and drove off happily, filled with admiration for his auntie. She was a sly one, Auntie Martha was. Thursday, she'd said.

'Unless I phones you otherwise. And I'll use a public phone. I've heard they can trace calls from homes and suchlike, the police can. Can't be too careful. I'll say . . .' She looked at the calendar with the kitten on the wall. 'I'll say Thursday 7th or 14th or whatever Thursday you're to do it. And that's all.'

'Why Thursday?' Bert asked.

'Cos that's when they play bridge at the Country Club till after midnight and he gets so drunk she can do what she likes with him and she don't go home till 4 or 5 in the morning. You'll have time enough to do what I told you.'

Bert drove past the Manor House, checked the lane behind it and then drove north with the map Martha Meadows had given him. He paused for a moment outside the Rottecombes' house, Leyline Lodge, and decided to come down again and make sure he knew exactly where to go. He'd borrow a friend's car for that trip too. He'd learnt a lot from Martha and he didn't want to get her into trouble.

8

Eva was not having a wonderful time. What she was going through was keeping her wide awake with worry half the night. After the effusive greetings at the airport from Uncle Wally and Auntie Joan and their delight at seeing the quads again, they had driven out to the private jet bearing the logo of Immelmann Enterprises and had climbed aboard. The jet had been cleared for take-off and presently they were flying west towards Wilma. Below them the landscape was dotted with lakes and rivers and after a while they were over woods and hills, with signs of habitation few and far between. The quads peered out of the windows and to satisfy their curiosity Uncle Wally put the jet into a dive and levelled out quite low down so that they could see the ground even better. Eva, who wasn't accustomed to flying and had never been up in a small plane before, felt queasy and frightened. But at least the girls were enjoying the ride and Uncle Wally was enjoying showing off his flying skills to them.

'She isn't as fast as the jets I flew in the Air Force out of Lakenheath, England,' he said, 'but she's good and manoeuvrable and she covers the ground fast enough for an old man like me.'

'Oh, shoot, honey, you ain't old,' Auntie Joan said. 'I

49

don't like you using that word. Everybody's just as old as they feel and the way you feel, Wally, feels pretty good and young to me. How's Henry these days, Eva?'

'Oh, Henry's just fine,' said Eva, readily adapting to American.

'Henry's a great guy,' said Wally. 'You got the makings of a great man there, Evie, you know that? I guess you girls are mighty proud of your daddy, eh? Having a daddy who's a professor is really something.'

Penelope began the process of disillusionment.

'Dad's not ambitious,' she said. 'He drinks too much.'

Wally said nothing but the plane dipped a little.

'A guy's got a right to a little liquor after a hard day's work,' he said. 'That's what I always say, isn't it, Joanie honey?'

Auntie Joan's smile suggested that that was indeed exactly what he always said. It also suggested disapproval.

'I gave up smoking though,' Wally said. 'Man, that stuff kills you and no mistake. Feel a hundred and ten per cent better since I quit.'

'Dad's taken up smoking again,' Samantha told him. 'He smokes a pipe because he says everyone is against smoking and no one is going to tell him what to do and what not to do.'

The plane dipped again.

'He really says that? Henry really says that? That no one is going to tell him what not to do?' said Wally, glancing nervously over his shoulder at the two women.

'Would you credit that? And he ain't much to look at manhoodwise either.'

'Wally!' said Auntie Joanie and there was no mistaking her meaning.

'And you stop speaking about Daddy like that,' Eva told Samantha with equal firmness.

'Hell, I didn't mean nothing by it,' said Wally. 'Manhood is just an expression.'

'Yeah, and yours isn't anything to write home about either,' said Auntie Joanie. 'Cracks like that just aren't called for.'

Uncle Wally said nothing. They flew on and finally Josephine spoke up.

'Boys aren't the only people with manhoods,' she said. 'I've got a sort of manhood too. It's not a very big one though. It's called a—'

'Shut up!' Eva shouted. 'We don't want to hear. Do you hear me, Josephine? Nobody's interested.'

'But Miss Sprockett said it was quite normal and some women prefer—' A swift cuff from Eva ended this exposition of Miss Sprockett's opinion of the function of the clitoris in one-to-one encounters between women. All the same it was clear that Uncle Wally was still interested.

'Gee, Miss Sprockett? That's some name for a woman.'

'She's our biology teacher and she's not like most women,' Samantha told him. 'She believes in practising masturbation. She says it's safer than having sex with men.'

51

This time there could be no doubting Wally's shock or the aerodynamic effect of Eva's sudden attempt to reach Samantha and shut her up. As the plane lurched, Wally fought to control it and wasn't helped by the blow on the side of his head intended for Samantha who had seen it coming and had ducked.

'Shit!' shouted Wally. 'For Chrissake everyone sit still. You want to ditch this kite?'

Even Auntie Joanie was alarmed. 'Eva, do sit down!' she yelled.

Eva sat back in her seat with a grim look on her face. Everything she had hoped to prevent was beginning to happen. She sat looking lividly at Samantha and willed her to go dumb at least temporarily. She was going to have to give the quads a good talking-to. For the rest of the flight there was a grim silence in the aircraft and an hour later they touched down at the little airfield at Wilma. The Immelmann Enterprises stretch limo in red and gold was waiting for them. So, discreetly hidden in an unmarked car, were two men from the Drug Enforcement Agency who watched as the Wilt children climbed out of the plane. In the back sat a local cop.

'You reckon?'

'Could be. Sam said they were in the same row 'longside the guy Sol Campito. Who's the fat guy?'

'Hell, that's Wally Immelmann. Runs the biggest plant in Wilma.'

'Anything on him? Like he's done time inside.'

'On Wally? Hell no, he's clean as you can be in his

business,' said the cop. 'Solid citizen. Pays his dues. Votes Republican and subscribes to everything he can. Backed Herb Reich for Congress.'

'So that makes him clean?'

'I didn't say he was clean as a hound's tooth. Just that he's a big wheel round these parts. I don't see him into drug running.'

'Just another fucking good ole boy? That right?' said the DEA man who was clearly not a Southerner.

'I guess so. I don't mix in those circles. I mean, man, that's money.'

'And how's his business doing right now?'

'Same as everything in Wilma. Pretty average, I guess. I don't know. He downsized last year but the latest is he's diversifying into things outside vacuum pumps.'

'So he could be . . . Shit, look at the one with the obesity problem.'

'That's his wife, Mrs Immelmann,' said the cop.

'Yeah, well it would be, wouldn't it? Who's the other one needs liposuction?'

The second DEA man checked the file.

'Name of Wilt, Mrs Eva Wilt, mother of the four pack, 45 Oakhurst Avenue, Ipford, England. Want to put out a check call on her?'

'They were in the same row with Sol. Could be he was the decoy. Yeah, call Atlanta and they can decide.'

They watched as the limo drove off. After it had gone the local cop got out and drove down to the Sheriff's office.

'What's with those drug-busting shits?' asked the Sheriff who resented Northerners almost as much as he resented being bossed around by the Feds. 'Come marching into Wilma like they own the whole fucking place.'

'You ain't going to believe this. They got Wally Immelmann tagged for a drug dealer.'

The Sheriff stared at him. The man was right. He didn't believe him.

'Wally into running drugs? You got to be joking! Oh my God, they must be out of their fucking heads. If Wally got to hear he was on a fucking dealer suspicion list he'd go apeshit. Would he ever. Like we got Mount St Helens volcano right here in Wispoen County spewing brimstone. Jesus.' He stopped and pondered for a moment. 'What evidence they got?'

'The fatso with the four girls. Dogs picked them out at the airport. And Wally is moving into pharmaceuticals. It fits.'

'And the woman? Why not hold her for questioning?'

'I don't know. Wanted to see her contact, I guess. British. Name of Wilt.'

The Sheriff groaned.

'Where those two goons from, Herb?' he said presently.

'Unit down Atlanta. They—'

'I got that already. Like, where are they from? What's their names and their home towns?'

'Don't give no names, Sheriff. Flash their IDs and

credentials from Drug Enforcement and come to the high and mighty. Those boys in that game don't have real names. Not good for their health, I've heard. Got numbers. One's from New Jersey, that I do know.'

'New Jersey? So how come the Yankee's doing duty down South? Don't trust us local cops?'

'They don't do that, and that's for sure. Wanted to know if Mr Immelmann was a good ole boy like it was a dirty word.'

'Said that, did they?' said the Sheriff grimly. 'Nice manners these Northern assholes have got. Come on down and think they run the place.'

'And the other one . . . name of Palowski, yeah that's right. I saw that much. He said Mrs Immelmann was so fat she should be into liposuction. Like that was a dirty word too.'

'It is,' said the Sheriff. 'OK, OK. They want to walk into a fire-storm with Wally Immelmann, I'm not going to stop them. They're on their own from now on. We just say Yessir and Nossir and let the bastards fuck up real good.'

'No cooperation, sir?'

The Sheriff sat back in his chair and smiled meaning-fully.

'Let's just say we let them draw their own conclusions. Ain't our asses going to be gored if they hit Wally. Good ole boy indeed. I reckon he'll good ole boy them so fast they won't have time to shit themselves.'

9

For five days Wilt wandered happily along little country
lanes, across fields, through woods, down bridle-paths
and beside streams and rivers, doing what he had hoped
to do: discover a different England remote from the
traffic and ugliness of big cities and the sort of life he led
in Ipford. At midday he would stop at a pub and have a
couple of pints and a sandwich and in the evening find
some small hotel or B & B where he could get a square
meal and a room for the night. The prices were
reasonable and the food varied but he wasn't looking for
anything modern or luxurious and the people were
friendly and helpful. In any case, he was always so tired –
he'd never done so much walking in his life before – that
he didn't care whether a bed was comfortable or not. And
when one landlady insisted rather unpleasantly that he
take his muddy boots off and not make a mess of her
carpets, he wasn't bothered. Nor did he ever feel lonely.
He'd come away to be alone, and apart from a few old
men in pubs who struck up conversations with him and
asked him where he was heading, and were puzzled when
he replied that he had no idea, he spoke to hardly anyone.
And the fact was that he really had no idea where he was
or where he was going. He deliberately didn't want to

know. It was enough to lean on a five-bar gate and watch a farmer on a tractor mowing hay, or to sit by a river in the sunshine and stare at the water drifting by. Once he glimpsed a dark shape glide through the grass on the far bank and disappear into the river, and supposed it must be an otter. Occasionally, when he had had rather more than his usual two pints of beer for lunch, he would find a sheltered spot behind a hedge and, having made sure there were no cattle in the field (he was particularly worried about meeting a bull), he would lean his head against the knapsack and snooze for half an hour before going on. There was never any need to hurry; he could take all the time in the world because he was going nowhere.

So it continued until on the sixth day the weather turned nasty in the late afternoon. The landscape had changed too and Wilt found himself crossing a stretch of spongy heath land with marshy areas he had to avoid. Several miles ahead there were some low hills but the emptiness and silence of the place had something faintly ominous about it and for the first time he began to feel faintly uneasy. It was almost as though he was being followed but when he looked back, as he did every now and then, there was nothing menacing in sight and no cover for anything to hide in. All the same the silence oppressed him and he hurried on. And then it began to rain. Thunder rumbled over the wooded hillside behind him and occasionally he caught a flash of lightning. The rain began to lash down, the lightning grew closer and

Wilt got out his anorak and wished it lived up to its maker's promise that it was waterproof. Shortly afterwards he blundered into a waterlogged area where he slipped and sat down in the muddy water with a squelch. Wet and miserable he hurried on still faster, conscious that the lightning was now very close. By this time he was near to the low rise beyond which he could see the tops of trees. Once there he would at least find some shelter. It took him half an hour and by then he was wet through, wet and cold and thoroughly uncomfortable. He was also hungry. For once he had failed to find a pub and have some lunch. Finally he was in the wood and had slumped down against the trunk of an old oak tree. The crash of lightning and the roll of thunder were the closest he had ever been to a storm and he was frankly frightened. He rummaged in his knapsack and found the bottle of Scotch he'd brought for emergencies. And in Wilt's opinion his present situation definitely came into the category of an emergency. Above him the darkening sky was made darker still by the clouds, and the wood itself was a dark one. Wilt swigged from the bottle, felt better and swigged again. Only then did it occur to him that sheltering under a tree was the worst thing to do in a thunderstorm. He no longer cared. He was not going back to that eerie heath with its bogs and waterlogged pools.

By the time he'd swigged several more times from the bottle he was feeling almost philosophical. After all, if one came on a walking tour to nowhere in particular and without really adequate preparations, one had to expect these sudden changes in the weather. And the storm was passing. The wind was beginning to fall. The branches of the trees above him no longer thrashed around and the lightning and thunder had moved on. Wilt counted the seconds between the flash and the thunder. Someone had once told him each second represented one mile. Wilt drank some more to celebrate the fact that by that calculation the eye of the storm was six miles away. But still the rain continued. Even under the oak it ran down his face. Wilt no longer cared. Finally, when the seconds between flash and crash had reached ten, he put the bottle away in the knapsack and got to his feet. He had to push on. He couldn't spend the night in the wood or, if he did, he'd be likely to go down with a bout of pneumonia. It was only when he'd managed to get the knapsack on his back – and this took some doing – and he took a few steps forward, that he realised how drunk he was. Drinking neat whisky on an empty stomach hadn't been at all sensible. Wilt tried to see what time it was but it was too dark to see the face of his watch. After half an hour during which he had twice fallen over logs, he sat down again and got out the bottle. If he was going to spend the night soaked to the skin in the middle of some benighted wood he might as well get thoroughly pissed. Then to his surprise he saw the lights of a vehicle through the trees to his left. It was a good distance away but at least it indicated that civilisation in the shape of a road existed down there. Wilt had begun to value civilisation. He stuffed the bottle into the pocket of the anorak and set off again. He had to reach that road and be near people. He no longer cared if he couldn't find a village. A barn or even a pigsty would do as well as a B & B. Just somewhere to lie down and sleep was enough for him now and in the morning he would be able to see where he was going. For the moment it was impossible. Weaving his way downhill he banged into trees and blundered through bracken but he made progress. Then suddenly his foot caught in the root of a thorn tree and he was falling head first into space. For a moment his knapsack, caught in the thorn, almost stopped his progress. Wilt continued falling, landed on his head in the back of Bert Addle's pick-up and passed out. It was Thursday night.

Across the lane and a field, Bert Addle was watching Meldrum Manor from the gate to the walled garden. He had driven down in a pick-up he'd borrowed from a mate who'd gone to Ibiza for a spree of drugs and booze and, if he had any energy left, some sex and a few fights. Bert was beginning to wonder if the lights in the house would ever go out and the bastard Battleby and Mrs Rottecombe go off to the Country Club. All he had to do now was get the keys from the beam in the barn and let himself in through the kitchen door when Battleby left. Finally at 10.45 the lights went out and he saw the couple shut the back door and drive off. Bert waited to make sure they'd had enough time to get to the Country Club. He'd already put on a pair of surgical gloves and half an hour later he was inside the kitchen and using his torch upstairs to find the cupboard in the passage opposite the bedroom. It was precisely where Martha had told him and in it were the things he needed. He went downstairs with them and found the plastic garbage bin in the kitchen. He pulled it away from the sink, and put some oily rags and a gumboot he'd brought with him in it. 'There's got to be plenty of smoke to attract the Fire Brigade,' Aunt Martha had told him and Bert meant to see that she got what she wanted. The gumboot would smoke and smell to high heaven as well. But first he had to move the Range Rover out of the yard and put the porno mags and some of the other S & M equipment in the front seat. That done and the Range Rover's doors locked he returned to the kitchen and lit the oily rag. As it began to smoulder he went out through the back door, took the keys out of his pocket and locked it. He whipped across the yard into the barn and put them back on the beam. Then he was running back to the pick-up, threw the hood and two whips and a couple of porn magazines into the back and drove up the lane to the road a mile beyond. His next visit had to be Leyline Lodge. The Rottecombes' house was two miles further on and conveniently secluded. No lights were on. Bert drove on, stopped, got out and reached over the back to get the whips and hood and was horrified to feel Wilt's leg. For a moment he questioned his own findings. A man lying in the back of the pick-up? When had the bastard got in? Must have been in the lane. Bert wasn't wasting any more time. He threw the S & M gear into the back garage, let down the back of the pick-up and hauled Wilt out with a thump on to the concrete floor. Then he was in the driver's seat and had left Leyline Lodge in a hurry. It was a wise move.

At Meldrum Manor Mrs Meadows's hopes that smoke would attract the attention of the Fire Brigade had exceeded her wildest dreams. They'd exceeded her worst fears as well. She had failed to take the Filipino maid's extravagant taste in exotic and extremely pungent air fresheners, and Battleby's detestation of them, into account. The previous morning he had hurled six pressurised cans of Jasmine Flower, Rose Blossom and Oriental Splendour into the garbage bin and told her never to get any more. As a result of Bert Addle's activities they wouldn't be needed. The smoke he had found so satisfying when the gumboot began to smoulder had slowly but surely turned into a raging fire. By the time it had reached the pressurised cans the Oriental Splendour lived up to its name and exploded. The other cans followed suit. With a roar that hurled flaming plastic across the kitchen and blew out the windows they announced to Meldrum Slocum that the Manor was on fire.

In her cottage Martha Meadows was busily providing herself with an alibi. She'd spent the earlier part of the evening as usual in the Meldrum Arms and had then invited Mr and Mrs Sawlie round for a spot of sloe gin she'd made the winter before. They were sitting comfortably in front of the telly when the cans exploded.

'Someone's car has backfired,' said Mrs Sawlie.

'Sounded more like a grenade to me,' said her husband. Mr Sawlie had been in the War. Five minutes later the overheated gas bottle for the kitchen stove reached bursting point. This time there could be no doubt that something closely resembling a bomb had gone off. A red glow in the direction of the Manor was followed by flames.

'Gawd help us,' said Mr Sawlie. 'The Manor's on fire. Best call the Fire Brigade.'

There was no need. In the distance came the sound of Fire Engines. The Sawlies crowded out into the street to watch the blaze. Behind them Martha Meadows helped herself to a very large sloe gin. What if Bert had got himself killed? She gulped down the gin and prayed.

10

At Meldrum Manor the firemen fought the blaze in vain. The fire had spread from the kitchen to the rest of the house and they had been delayed by the Range Rover in the gate of the back yard. In the end they had been forced to break a side window to unlock the door and the car alarm had gone off. More delay and the discovery of the S & M mags and equipment on the front seat. By the time the police arrived the source of the fire had been discovered.

'As clear a case of arson as I've ever seen,' the Fire Chief told the Superintendent when he arrived. 'Not a shred of doubt about it, not in my mind at any rate. The investigators will get the full evidence. Plastic dustbin in the middle of the room and a wall cupboard full of spray cans. The bloke must have been mad to think he could get away with it.'

'There's no chance it could have been an accident?'

'All the doors locked and the windows blown outwards and it's an accident? Not on your nelly.'

'The windows blown outwards?'

'Like a bomb went off. And some people in the village saw the fireball. Besides, whoever set this little lot going, had a key to the house. Like I said the bloke had to be mad or drunk.'

The Superintendent was thinking the same thing only more so. Mad and drunk.

'And take a dekko at what's in the Range Rover,' said the Fire Chief. They went down to the road and looked at the magazines on the front seat. 'I've seen some filth in my time – people keep some pretty foul porn in their houses – but never anything like this. Bloke ought to be prosecuted. Not my business, of course.'

The Superintendent looked at the magazines and agreed about prosecuting. He had in mind a charge of being in Possession of Obscene Material. He didn't like porn at the best of times but when it involved sadism and little children he was savage. He didn't like leather straps and handcuffs either.

'You didn't touch anything?' he asked.

'Wouldn't if you paid me. I've got kids of my own, leastways my daughters have. I'd flog the bastards who do that sort of thing.'

The Superintendent agreed. He'd never seen porn as foul as this lot. In any case, he didn't like Bob Battleby one little bit. The man had a rotten reputation and a vile temper. And the clear indication of arson was very interesting indeed. Rumour had it that Battleby had lost a small fortune gambling on the stock market and had been living off cash the General's wife had left him. He'd have to look into Battleby's financial position. There was talk that he was seen too often in the company of the local MP's wife, Ruth Rottecombe, and the Superintendent didn't like her one little bit either. On the other hand, the

Battlebys had influence – and Members of Parliament, particularly Shadow Ministers and their wives, had to be handled with kid gloves. He looked at the gag and the handcuffs and shook his head. There were some real weirdos and swine in the world.

On the road in front of the house Bob Battleby stared in disbelief at the smouldering shell that had been the family home for over two hundred years. The news that the Manor was on fire had reached him at the Country Club and, being even drunker than usual, he had greeted it with disbelief. The Club Secretary had to be joking.

'Pull the other one. It can't be. There's no one there.'

'You had better speak to the Fire Brigade yourself,' the Secretary told him. He disliked Battleby when he was sober. The man was an arrogant snob and invariably rude. When he was drunk and had lost money in a game of poker he was infinitely worse.

'You had better be right, bloody right,' Battleby told him threateningly. 'If this is a false alarm, I'll see you get the fucking sack and . . .'

But whatever he'd meant to say was left unsaid. He slumped into a chair and dropped his glass. Mrs Rottecombe took the call in the Secretary's office and heard the news of the fire apparently without emotion. She was a hard woman and her association with Bob Battleby was based solely on self-interest.

In spite of his drinking and his general arrogance he was socially useful. He was a Battleby and the family name counted a great deal when it came to votes. Influence and power mattered to Ruth Rottecombe. She had married Harold Rottecombe shortly after he was first elected to Parliament and she had sensed he was an ambitious man who only needed a strong woman behind him to succeed. Ruth saw herself as just such a woman. She did what had to be done and had no scruples. Self-preservation came first in her mind and sex didn't come into her marriage. She'd had enough sex in her younger days. Power was all that mattered now. Besides, Harold was away in Westminster all week and she was sure he had his own peculiar sexual inclinations. What was important was that he kept his safe seat in Parliament and remained a Shadow Minister and, if that meant keeping in with Bob Battleby and satisfying his sado-masochistic fantasies by tying him up and whipping him on Thursday nights, she was perfectly prepared to do it. In fact, she got considerable satisfaction from the act. It was better than staying at home and being bored to death by all the inane activities like hunting and shooting and attending bridge parties and coffee mornings and talking about gardening that country life seemed to involve. So she took her two bull terriers for walks and was careful not to dress too smartly. And by acting as Bob's driver and minder she supposed his family must be grateful to her. Not that she had any illusions about what they really thought of her. As she put it to herself, they owed her, and one day when she was safely installed in London and the Government had a really solid majority she would see to it that they paid her back with due deference.

But now as she put the phone down she had the feeling that a crisis was looming. If Bob, through some act of drunken carelessness like leaving a pan on the stove, had set the Manor on fire, there would be hell to pay. She left the office thoughtfully and went back to him.

'I'm sorry, Bob, but it is true. The house is on fire. We'd better go.'

'On fire? Can't bloody be. It's a listed building. Built two hundred years ago. Houses that old don't catch fire. Not like the modern rubbish they put up nowadays.'

Mrs Rottecombe ignored the implied insult to her own house and with the Club Secretary's help got him up from the chair and out to her Volvo estate.

It was only now as he stood swaying in the roadway surrounded by fire hoses and stared at the smoking shell of the beautiful house – fires were burning in the interior and being doused by the firemen when they flared up again – that some sense of reality returned to Beastly Battleby.

'Oh God, what are the family going to say?' he whined. 'I mean, the family portraits and everything. Two Gainsboroughs and a Constable. And the fucking furniture. Oh shit! And they weren't insured.'

He was either sweating profusely or weeping. It was difficult in the dim light to tell which. He was still drunk and maudlin. Mrs Rottecombe said nothing. She had despised him before; now she had nothing but utter contempt. She should never have associated with the wimp.

'It was probably the wiring,' she said finally. 'When did you have it rewired last?'

'Rewired? I don't know. Twelve or thirteen years ago. Something like that. Nothing wrong with the bloody wiring.'

They were interrupted by the police Superintendent.

'A terrible tragedy, Mr Battleby. A tragic loss.'

Battleby turned and looked at him belligerently. A sudden flare-up in what had been the library illuminated his suffused face.

'What's it got to do with you? Not your bloody loss,' he said.

'Not mine personally, no, sir. I meant for you and the county, sir.'

The Superintendent's deference was tinged with hidden anger. He would lard his questions with 'sirs' and take his time. No need to get up Mrs Rottecombe's nose. On the other hand, now was the time to see Battleby's reaction to the filth in the Range Rover.

'I wonder if you'd mind stepping round to the back, sir?'

'What the hell for? Why don't you just bugger off. It's not your fucking house.'

Mrs Rottecombe intervened. 'Now, Bob, the Inspector is only trying to help.'

The Superintendent ignored his demotion. 'It's a question of identification, sir,' he said and watched carefully.

Mrs Rottecombe was shocked but the drunken

Battleby misunderstood. 'What the fuck! You know me already. Known me for bloody years.'

'Not you, sir,' the Superintendent said and paused significantly. 'There's something else.'

'Something else, Chief Superintendent?' Mrs Rottecombe corrected her previous mistake. There was genuine anxiety in her voice now.

The Superintendent took advantage of it. He nodded slowly and added, 'A bad business, I'm afraid. Not at all pleasant.'

'Surely not someone dead . . .'

The Superintendent didn't reply. He led the way round to the Range Rover, stepping over hose-pipes and with the acrid smell of smoke in their nostrils. Battleby stumbled after them. Mrs Rottecombe wasn't helping him now. The smell and the Superintendent's sinister emphasis was playing on her imagination. In the darkness the Range Rover might have been an ambulance. Several policemen stood nearby. Only when they got closer did she see it was Bob's vehicle. So did he and protested.

'What the devil's it doing out here?' he demanded.

The Superintendent answered with his own question. 'I assume you always keep it locked, sir?'

'Of course I do. I'm not a damned fool. Don't want it stolen, do I?'

'And you locked it tonight, sir?'

'What do you think? Asking dumb questions like that,' said Battleby. 'Of course I locked it.'

'Just making sure, sir. You see, the firemen had to

break the side window to move it out into the road, sir.'
There could be no mistaking the purpose of the repeated
'sir', at least not for Mrs Rottecombe. It was intended to
provoke and it succeeded.

'What the fuck did they do that for? That's breaking
and entering. They had no right to—'

'Because you had locked it, sir, as you have just
admitted. The fire engines couldn't get into the yard, sir,'
said the Superintendent. More provocation. He said it
slowly as though explaining the matter to a backward
child. 'And now, sir, if you'd be so good as to give me the
keys I'll—'

But Battleby had been baited far enough. 'Oh, fuck off,
copper,' he said, 'and mind your own business. My
bloody house burns to the ground and all you want to do
is—'

'Give him the keys, Bob,' said Mrs Rottecombe firmly.
Battleby swore again and groped in his pockets and finally
found them. He tossed them towards the Superintendent
who picked them off the ground and made a show of
unlocking the door on the passenger's side.

'If you wouldn't mind, sir, I'd like you to look at this
material, sir,' he said, blocking Mrs Rottecombe's view
and switching on the interior light. Lying on the seat
beside the gag and the handcuffs were the magazines.
The Superintendent stood back and let Battleby see
them. For a moment he gaped at them.

'Who the fuck put them there?'

'I was hoping you could tell me that, sir,' said the

Superintendent and moved away so that Mrs Rottecombe could see the collection. Her reaction was more informative. It was also more calculated.

'Oh, Bob, how revolting! Where on earth did you buy that filth?'

Battleby turned his bloated face on her lividly. 'Where did I buy it? I didn't buy it anywhere. I don't know what it's doing there.'

'Are you saying someone gave it to you, sir? If so, would you mind telling me who—'

'No, I'm fucking not,' Battleby shouted, totally losing control of his temper. Mrs Rottecombe backed away from him. She knew now that she had to distance herself from him. Being the friend of a man who had pictures of children being raped and tortured was the last thing she needed. Tying Bob up and whipping him was one thing but sadistic paedophilia . . . And the police were definitely involved now. She wanted out. The Superintendent took a step closer to Battleby and peered into his purple face and bloodshot eyes.

'If you didn't buy this material and no one gave it to you, just tell me how it happens to be in your car, your locked car, sir. You tell me that. You're not suggesting it got in there by itself, are you, sir?'

There was no doubting his sarcasm now. This was interrogation proper. Mrs Rottecombe made an attempt to get away.

'If you don't mind . . .' she began but the Superintendent's tactics had achieved the object he had been hoping for. Battleby took a drunken swig at his face. The Superintendent made no attempt to dodge the blow; it struck him full on the nose and blood ran down his chin. He was almost smiling. The next moment Battleby's arms were behind his back, he was handcuffed and a large Sergeant was frogmarching him to a police car.

'I think we had better continue this interview in a calmer atmosphere,' said the Superintendent, not bothering to wipe the blood from his face. 'I'm afraid you'll have to accompany us too, Mrs Rottecombe. I know it's very late but we'll need a statement from you. It's not just a case of assaulting a police officer in the course of his duty. There's Possession of Obscene Material under the Act as well. You were a witness to everything that occurred. And there is another matter, possibly a more serious one.'

Mrs Rottecombe crossed to her Volvo and followed the police cars to the police station in Oston in a state of controlled fury. Bob Battleby was going to get no help from her.

11

'You're not going to like this, Flint,' Superintendent Hodge of the Drug Squad in Ipford said with all the glee of a man who was finally being proved right, and that at the expense of a man he thoroughly disliked. He settled his backside on the edge of Inspector Flint's desk to emphasise the point.

'Don't see how I am,' said Flint. 'Don't tell me they're putting you back on the beat. I mean, that would really hurt me.'

The Superintendent smiled nastily. 'Remember what you told me about Wilt not being into drugs? Said the blighter wasn't that sort. Well, I've got news for you. The Drug Enforcement Agency in the States has faxed an inquiry on Mrs Wilt in a drug-dealing connection. What do you say to that?'

'I'd say you'd picked up some fancy transatlantic language. Been seeing too many old movies, have you? The Wilt Connection. You've got to be joking.'

'They are requesting information about Mrs Eva Wilt, address 45 Oakhurst Avenue—'

'I know where the Wilts live, don't I just,' said Flint. 'But if you are trying to tell me that Eva Wilt is into drug pushing you're clean round the twist. That woman is a leading anti-drug campaigner like she's a leading campaigner for everything else from Save the Whales to stopping the TV cable company from digging holes along Oakhurst Avenue because it hurts the cherry trees and they are part of the Ipford Rainforest. Pull the other one.'

Hodge ignored the crack. 'Of course she's a leading anti-drug campaigner. Gives her splendid cover Stateside.'

Inspector Flint sighed. Really, Superintendent Hodge was getting to be a bigger fool the more he was promoted.

'Where are we now? *Kojak*? You should watch something a bit more up to date than that old stuff. Not that I mind. At least I can sort of understand what you're talking about.'

'Very witty, I'm sure,' said Hodge. 'So if she's so clean how come they're asking for information?'

'Don't ask me what Yanks do. I've never understood. Anyway, what reason did they give?'

'Presumably because they have her under suspicion,' said Hodge and moved off the desk. 'Our American confrères don't give reasons. All they're doing is asking. Makes you think, doesn't it?'

'Be nice if some people could begin to,' said Flint when the door closed behind the Superintendent. 'And what was all that confrères business about?'

'I think he was just trying to show he can speak a bit of French as well as American,' said Sergeant Yates. 'Though what a confrère is, I'm blowed if I know.'

'Means the cunt of my brother,' said the Inspector.

'But men don't have cunts.'

'I know that, Sergeant, but try telling that to Hodge. He is one.'

He went back to more urgent cases than Eva Wilt pushing drugs only to be interrupted by Sergeant Yates.

'Beats me how he ever got back into the Drug Squad after he fouled up the last time. Promoted to Superintendent too.'

'Think sex, Yates, think sex, and influence and wedding bells. Married the ugliest woman in Ipford like the Mayor's sister. That's how. I thought even you knew that. Now let me get on with some work.'

'The slimy shit,' said the Sergeant and left the office.

In Wilma, Sheriff Stallard's attitude towards the DEA agents was much the same. 'They've got to be crazy,' he told his Deputy over coffee in the local drugstore when Baxter reported that five more agents had booked into a nearby motel and that there was already a tap on Wally Immelmann's phone line. 'He'll raise Cain when he gets to know.'

'Bugging the house is the next phase,' said Baxter. 'They're moving in at the weekend when he's going up to the lake house.'

The Sheriff made a mental note to be out of town over the weekend. He wasn't going to take the rap for bugging Wally Immelmann's mansion or even knowing about it. He'd visit his mother down in Birmingham in the nursing home.

'You don't know nothing about this, Baxter,' he said.

'You haven't told me and they never told you. We could be in deep shit if we don't take good care of ourselves. You got anyone could do with arresting on Saturday?'

'Saturday? There's that punk up Roselea beats the shit out of his wife Friday nights.'

'Need someone better than that,' the Sheriff told him. 'How about picking up Hank Veblen for the burglarising job he did last month and grilling him all Saturday Sunday. Keep you busy doing that.'

'Yeah, I reckon Hank could do with some questioning,' Baxter agreed. 'But he'll call his lawyer and get sprung too quick. He's got an alibi.'

'Got to be someone in town needs grilling. Think about it, Herb. You're going to need an alibi yourself if those goons go into the Starfighter with bugs.'

'Bound to be trouble Saturday someplace. I'll find a reason.'

Uncle Wally's mind was working along the same lines. The prospect of going up to Lake Sassaquassee with Eva and the four girls was not one that had the greatest appeal for him.

'I tell you, Joanie, I got premonitions about them. You told me they were real nice. Cute, you said. Well, cute they ain't. Not my sort of cute. Four fucking hell-cats is what they are. That one called Penny's been round asking questions of Maybelle and the rest of the help.'

'What sort of questions, honey? I didn't hear about that.'

'Like what we pay her and does she get enough time off and do we treat her right?'

'Oh, that. Eva told me they'd be interested. They've been given a school project on life in the US.'

'School project? What sort of school is it wants to know what the minimum wage is and do I screw her often?'

Even Auntie Joan was shocked.

'Wally, she didn't ask Maybelle that? Oh, my God. Maybelle's a Deaconess in her church and real religious. They go round asking her things like that she's going to walk out on us.'

'That's what I'm telling you. And that's not all. Rube says they wanted to know how many gays there are in Wilma, what proportion of the town and if they're black or white and living together as married folk. In Wilma! That gets out it won't just be Maybelle leaves. I'll be going too.'

'Oh Wally,' said Auntie Joan and sat down heavily on the bed. 'What are we going to do?'

Wally gave the matter some thought. 'I guess we'd better go up the lake after all. There's no one they can ask anything of up there. And you tell that Eva she's got to stop them before it gets out what they're doing. How many mixed couples of gays in Wilma? Jesus, that beats everything.'

It didn't. That afternoon Auntie Joan had invited the Revd and Mrs Cooper over with their daughters to meet her nieces. The occasion was not a success. The Reverend enquired what they learnt about God at their school in England. Auntie Joan tried to intervene but it was no good. Samantha had summed the Revd Cooper up only too accurately.

'God?' she asked in a bewildered tone of voice. 'Who is God?'

It was the turn of the Revd Cooper to look utterly bewildered. It was obvious that no one had ever put such a question to him before.

'God? Well, I'd have to say . . . I'd have to say . . .' he faltered.

Mrs Cooper took up the problem. 'God is love,' she said sanctimoniously.

The quads looked at her with new interest. This was going to be fun.

'Do you make God?' Emmeline asked.

'Make God? Did you say "make God"?' asked Mrs Cooper.

Auntie Joan smiled bleakly. She didn't know what was coming but she had an idea it wasn't going to make things easier. In fact it made things extremely unpleasant.

'You make love and if God is love you must make him,' said Emmeline with a seraphic smile. 'People wouldn't exist if you didn't make love. That's how babies are made.'

Mrs Cooper gazed at her in horror. She couldn't find any answer to that one.

The Revd Cooper could. 'Child,' he said loudly and injudiciously. 'You know not of what you speak. Those are the words of Satan. They are evil words.'

'They aren't. They're simple logic and logic isn't evil. You said God is love and I said—'

'We all heard what you said,' Eva said, drowning out the Revd Cooper. 'And we don't want to hear any more from you. Do you understand that, Emmy?'

'Yes, Mummy,' said Emmeline. 'But I still don't understand what God is.'

There was a long silence broken by Auntie Joan who wanted to know if anyone would like some more iced tea. The Revd Cooper silently prayed for guidance. The phrase 'out of the mouths of babes and sucklings' didn't apply. These four horrible girls weren't babes or sucklings. All the same he had his mission to pursue.

'It says in the Bible that God created the heaven and the earth. Genesis 1:1. We are all the children of God—' he began. Josephine interrupted. 'It must have made a terrible noise, the Big Bang,' she said, giving the word 'bang' a distinctly peculiar but unmistakably lubricious emphasis.

Eva had had enough. 'Go to your room at once!' she shouted as wrathfully as the Revd Cooper felt.

'I'm only trying to find out what God is,' said Josephine meekly.

Mrs Cooper struggled with conflicting feelings and decided that Southern hospitality should prevail. 'Oh, it's quite all right,' she cooed. 'I guess we all need to learn the truth.'

Eva doubted it. Auntie Joan clearly didn't look as if she

needed any more truth. A slug of liquor more like. Eva wasn't risking her having a stroke.

'I'm sorry,' she said to the Coopers, 'but they must go to their room. I'm not having any more rudeness from them.'

The quads filed out grumbling.

'I guess you have a different system of education in England,' said the Revd Cooper when they had gone. 'And I heard they have religious service in school first thing every morning. Seems they don't give them Bible reading or anything.'

'It isn't easy bringing four girls the same age up all together,' said Eva, in a desperate attempt to salvage something from the disaster. 'We have never been able to afford a nanny or anything like that.'

'Oh, you poor things,' said Mrs Cooper. 'My, how dreadful. You mean to say you all don't have servants in England? I wouldn't have believed it after seeing all those films with butlers and castles and all.' She turned to Auntie Joan. 'I guess you were lucky having the daddy you had, Joanie. A Lord who stayed with the Queen at Sandrin . . . that house you told me about where they go duck hunting. Why he'd just be bound to have a butler open the door for him and all. What was the name of the butler, you know the one who was so fat and drank port wine you told us about at the country club that time Sandra and Al had their silver anniversary?'

A strange, choking sound from Auntie Joan suggested that her condition had worsened. The afternoon was not a success. That evening Eva tried to put her fourth call through to Wilt. There was no answer. Eva went to bed that night and hardly slept. She knew now she should never have come. Wally and Auntie Joan knew that too.

'We'd better go up to the lake tomorrow,' he said helping himself to four fingers of bourbon. 'Get them out of the way.'

But as the quads were going to bed Josephine found what Sol Campito had pushed among the things in her hand luggage. It was a small sealed gelatine cylinder and she didn't like the look of it. The other girls didn't like the look of it either and swore they hadn't put it there.

'It could be something dangerous,' said Penelope.

'Like what?' asked Emmeline.

'Like a bomb.'

'It's too small for a bomb. And it's too soft. When you squeeze it—'

'Then don't. It might burst and we don't know what is in it.'

'Whatever it is I don't want it,' said Josephine.

Nobody wanted it. In the end they threw it out the window where it landed in the swimming-pool.

'Now if it's a bomb it won't do any harm,' said Emmeline.

'Unless Uncle Wally's taking his early-morning dip. He could be blown up.'

'Serve him right. He's a big mouth,' said Samantha.

12

By the time Ruth Rottecombe got to bed it was after 7 a.m. Her night had been an exceedingly unpleasant one. The police station at Oston was not a new one and while it might have held some quaint charm for old lags, it had held none whatsoever for Mrs Rottecombe. For one thing it smelt and the smells were all horrible and revoltingly unhygienic. Tobacco smoke mingled with the various foul by-products of far too many beers and too much fear and sweat. Even the Superintendent's attitude had changed once they were inside. His nose hadn't stopped bleeding and the police surgeon summoned from his bed to take blood from a man who had failed the breathalyser test was of the opinion that it might well have been broken. The Superintendent greeted this piece of information by ignoring Mrs Rottecombe's presence and giving vent to his feelings about 'that drunken bastard, Battleby' in several words of four letters. He also expressed his belief that the drunken swine had in all likelihood burnt his own house down for the insurance money.

'Doubt?' he had said with a muffled snarl through the bloodstained handkerchief. 'Doubt? Ask Robson, the Fire Chief. He'll tell you. A plastic dustbin in the middle of the kitchen catches fire of its own accord and all the doors locked? It's as plain as the nose . . . ouch. Wait till I've had him for forty-eight hours.'

At this point Mrs Rottecombe had asked faintly if she could sit down and the Superintendent regained some slight composure. It wasn't much. She might be the wife of the local MP but she was also the regular associate of a suspected arsonist and paedophile and the bastard who had broken his nose. One thing was certain, she wasn't above the Law. He'd show her that.

'You can go in there,' he said gruffly, indicating the office next door. Mrs Rottecombe then made the mistake of asking if she could use the toilet.

'Feel free,' he said and pointed down a passage. Five utterly horrifying minutes later, she emerged ashen. She had vomited twice and it was only by holding her nose with one hand while supporting herself against a wall smeared with excreta that she was able to avoid sitting down. Not that there was a seat but even if there had been she wouldn't have dreamt of sitting on it. In any case the water-closet didn't live up to its name.

'Are those the best toilet facilities you can provide?' she asked when she came back and instantly regretted it. The Superintendent raised his head. He had stuffed his nostrils with cotton wool and they were already a horrid red. His eyes weren't much pleasanter.

'I don't provide any facilities,' he said, sounding like a bad case of adenoids in a foul temper. 'The Local Authority does. Ask your husband. Now then, about your movements this evening. I understand from the other suspect that you habitually meet at the Country Club every Thursday night and . . . Well, would you care to explain your relationship with him?'

In the face of that 'the other suspect' Mrs Rottecombe drew on her reserves of arrogance. 'What's that got to do with you? I find the question highly irregular,' she said haughtily.

The Superintendent's nostrils flared. 'And I find your relationship irregular too, Mrs Rottecombe, not to say peculiar.'

Mrs Rottecombe stood up. 'How dare you address me in that manner?' she squawked. 'Do you know who I am?'

The Superintendent took a deep breath through his mouth and let it out with a snort through his nose. Two red blobs fell on to the blotter in front of him. He reached for some fresh cotton wool and took his time replacing them.

'Trying to pull social rank, are we? Coming the old high horse. It won't wash, not here and not with me. Now sit down or stand, just as you like, but you're going to answer some questions. First of all, did you know that "Bobby Beat Me" . . . Ah, I see you did know the locals' name for him. Well, your little friend is very interesting about Thursday nights. Calls it "Slap and Tickle Night" and would you be interested to know what he calls you? Ruthless mean anything to you, Ruth the Ruthless? Now, I wonder why he calls you that. Fits in with those filthy mags he's fond of. What do you say to that?'

What Mrs Rottecombe would have liked to say was unspeakable. 'I shall issue a writ for slander.'

The Superintendent smiled. There was blood on his teeth now. 'Very sensible of you. Nail the bastard. And after all they do say there's no such thing as bad publicity.' He paused and looked at his notes. 'Now, the fire, the actual fire that is known to have started just after midnight. Are you prepared to swear that at midnight you were in the company of the accused at the Club?'

'I was at the Club, yes, and Mr Battleby was there too. The Club Secretary can testify to that. I would not say I was in his company, as you put it.'

'In that case I suppose he drove himself there.'

Mrs Rottecombe tried to be patronising. 'My dear Superintendent, I assure you I had absolutely nothing to do with the fire. The first I knew about it was when the Secretary called me to the phone.'

That hadn't worked either. It had merely infuriated the Superintendent. As soon as she left he got the Sergeant to call the *News on Sunday* and the *Daily Rag* and give them the word that there was a story involving a Shadow Minister's wife to be had at Meldrum Slocum. A juicy story involving arson and sex. Having done that he went home. His nose had stopped bleeding.

She was therefore in no condition to be shaken awake at 8.30 by an obviously demented husband. She peered blearily up into his ashen face. His eyes seemed to be starting out of his head and had an awful intensity about them.

'What's the matter?' she mumbled blearily. 'What's happened, Harold?'

There was a moment's silence while the Shadow Minister for Social Enhancement struggled to control himself and his wife slowly realised that he must have heard about the fire at the Manor.

'Happened? Happened? You're asking me what's happened?' he yelled when he could bring himself to say anything.

'Well, yes, as a matter of fact I am. And please don't bawl like that. And what are you doing here? You usually come home on Friday night.'

Mr Rottecombe's vicelike hands twitched convulsively in front of her. He had a terrible impulse to strangle the bitch. Even Ruth could tell that. Instead he controlled the urge by ripping the bedclothes off the bed and hurling them on to the floor.

'Go and look in the fucking garage,' he snarled and dragged her by the arm out of bed. For the first time in her married life Ruth the Ruthless was afraid of him. 'Go on, you bitch. Go and see what you've landed us in this time. And you don't need a fucking dressing gown.'

Mrs Rottecombe put her feet into a pair of slippers and tottered downstairs to the kitchen. For a second she paused by the door into the garage.

'What's wrong in there?' she asked.

The question was too much for Harold. 'Don't just stand there. Go!' he bellowed.

Mrs Rottecombe went. For several minutes she stood staring down at Wilt's body, her mind desperately trying to come to grips with yet another disaster. By the time she returned she had come to one conclusion. For once in her life she was innocent and in the crude parlance of her youth, she wasn't going to take the can back. She found Harold sitting at the kitchen table with a large brandy. Ruth took advantage of his attitude.

'You don't seriously think I had anything to do with him being there,' she said. 'I've never seen the man in my life before.'

The statement galvanised her husband. He rose to his feet. 'I suppose it was too fucking dark,' he shouted. 'You pick up some poor bastard . . . Was that swine Battleby too drunk to satisfy your sadistic needs so you find that bloke and . . . Dear God!'

The telephone was ringing in the study.

'I'll answer it,' said Ruth, feeling slightly more in control.

'Well? Who was it?' he asked when she came back.

'Only the *News on Sunday*. They want to interview you.'

'Me? That filthy rag? What the hell about?'

Mrs Rottecombe took her time. 'I think we'd better have some coffee,' she said and busied herself at the stove with the electric kettle.

'Well, for goodness' sake, get on with it. What do they

want to interview me about?'

For a moment she hesitated before deciding where to strike. 'Only about your bringing young men into the house.'

For a moment Harold Rottecombe was left speechless. The word 'only' did the damage. Incredulity struggled with fury. Then the dam burst.

'I didn't bring the bastard into the house, for Christ's sake. You did. I've never brought any young men to the house. And anyway he isn't young. He's fifty if he's a day. I don't believe this. I'm not hearing right. I can't be.'

'I'm only telling you what the man said. He said "young men". And that's not all. He also mentioned "rent-boys",' said Mrs Rottecombe to deepen the crisis. It took the heat off her.

The MP's eyes bulged in his head. He looked as though he was going to have an apoplectic fit. For once his wife rather hoped he would. It would save a lot of very difficult explanations. Instead the phone in the hall rang again.

'I'll get it this time,' Harold yelled and stormed out of the kitchen. For a moment she heard him telling someone he'd already called a bugger to fuck off and leave him alone. Then she shut the door and poured herself a cup of coffee and planned her next move. Harold was a long time gone. He came back a chastened man.

'That was Charles,' he said grimly.

Mrs Rottecombe nodded. 'I thought it might be. Nothing like calling the Chairman of the Local Party a bugger and telling him to fuck off. And this was such a safe seat.'

The Member of Parliament for Otterton looked at her with loathing. Then he brightened up briefly and fought back. 'The good news is that your lover boy Battleby's been charged with assaulting a police officer and is being held in custody pending the more serious charges of possessing obscene material of a paedophile nature, and very possibly arson. Apparently Meldrum Manor was burnt to the ground last night.'

'I know,' said Mrs Rottecombe coolly. 'I saw it afterwards. Anyway, that's not our problem. He'll probably dry out in prison.'

The phone ran again. Stunned by his wife's insouciance, Harold let her answer it.

'*Daily Graphic* this time,' she announced when she returned. 'Wouldn't say why they wanted to interview you which means they're on the same track. Someone's been talking.'

Harold helped himself to another brandy with a shaking hand.

Mrs Rottecombe shook her head wearily. There were times – and this was one of them – when she wondered how a man with so little gumption had done so well as a politician. No wonder the country had gone to the dogs. The phone rang again.

'For heaven's sake don't answer it,' Harold said.

'Of course we've got to answer it. We can't be seen to have cut ourselves off from the world. Now just leave this to me,' she told him. 'You'll only make a mess of things by shouting.'

She went back to the phone and Harold hurried through to his study and picked up the extension on his desk.

'No, I'm afraid he's still in London,' he heard her say only to learn that the caller, a reporter from the *Weekly Echo*, had another source of information, and was she Mrs Rottecombe, wife of the Shadow Minister for Social Enhancement?

Mrs Rottecombe said coldly that she was.

'And at 4 a.m. you were in the company of a man called Battleby when the police seized some whips, a gag and handcuffs together with a quantity of paedophile S & M magazines in his possession?' It was less a question than a statement of fact.

Mrs Rottecombe lost her cool. And her head. 'That's a downright lie!' she shouted. Harold held the phone away from his ear. 'If you print that I'll sue for libel.'

'The source is good,' said the man. 'Very good. We've traced the call. This bloke Battleby's been charged. Got an arson rap against him too. Slugged a policeman. Source told us you've been giving "Bobby Beat Me" his medicine for some time. Like with whips and him hand-cuffed. Known as "Ruthless Ruth Rottecombe" locally, according to our information.'

Mrs Rottecombe slammed the phone down. Harold waited a moment and heard the reporter ask someone if they'd got that on tape. The answer was, 'Yes. And we've got a story too. He is the Shadow Minister for Social Enhancement. Juicy's the word and the bitch's reaction confirms the info we got from the cops.'

Harold Rottecombe replaced the extension. His hand was shaking uncontrollably now. His entire career was at stake. He went through to the kitchen.

'I knew this would happen!' he shouted. 'You have to get involved with the local piss artist . . . Beat Me Bobby and Ruth the Ruthless. Oh, God. And you have to threaten them with libel. What a bloody mess.' He helped himself to some cooking brandy. The other bottle was empty. Mrs Rottecombe eyed him icily. Power and influence were slipping away fast. She had to find a socially acceptable explanation for her actions. It was too late to deny she'd associated with the wretched Battleby but she could always claim she'd only done so to stop him losing his driving licence. Or was he simply a drunk? An idiot who could leave those porn mags in his Range Rover where they could be seen had to be out of his mind. And accidentally set fire to his own house? Ruth Rottecombe knew that full-blown alcoholics frequently behaved insanely and Bob had been blind drunk last night. That was undoubtedly true. He'd been mad enough to hit that Superintendent but all the same . . . Not that she cared about Battleby. She had herself to think of. And Harold. He was up to his eyebrows too but even so a Shadow Minister still had influence. At least for the moment. There had to be some way of using that influence in a damage-limitation exercise. Finally there was that unconscious man in the garage. Mrs Rottecombe applied her mind to the problem. She had to keep Harold out of the scandal. As the MP gulped the brandy his wife acted. She snatched the bottle from him.

'No more of that,' she snapped. 'You've got to drive back to London immediately and you'll be over the limit if you have any more. I'll stay here and deal with any further inquiries.'

'All right, I'll go, I'll go,' he said but it was already too late. A car had turned in to the drive and had pulled up outside the front door. Two men got out and one was carrying a camera. With a curse Harold Rottecombe dashed towards the back of the house and out across the lawn past the swimming-pool and over the low wall into the artificial ditch beyond it. He'd be hidden there. Ruth was right. He mustn't be known to have come back from London. He'd be off like a shot the moment they left. He sat down with his back to the wall and looked out across the rolling countryside with the dark thread of the river running in the distance down to the sea. It had all looked so peaceful before. It didn't now.

At the front door events were about to prove him right. Mrs Rottecombe's feelings for investigative journalists had developed from intense dislike to downright fury. She was followed by Wilfred and Pickles. The bull terriers had sensed the atmosphere of alarm that pervaded the house. There had been shouting downstairs, the telephone had rung rather more frequently than was normal and the master had used an expression they knew from bitter experience to mean trouble. As they stood beside her inside the front door they could smell her anger and fear.

13

Outside, the journalist and cameraman from the *News on Sunday* were less perceptive. In any case they were accustomed to annoying and terrifying the people they were sent to interview. Even by the standards of the gutter press the *News on Sunday* was held in awe by hardened editors and other newspaper men. It excelled in intrusive journalism. In short it purveyed pure sewage, and Butcher Cassidy and the Flashgun Kid, as the two reporters were aptly nicknamed by others in their profession, were sewer rats and proud of their reputation. They'd already made inquiries in Meldrum Slocum about Battleby and 'Ruthless Ruth' and had had an interesting chat with an off-duty policeman. After that they had decided on their usual brutish approach and had driven over to Leyline Lodge. A sign on the gate which read 'BEWARE OF THE DOG' hadn't deterred them for a moment. Over the years they had encountered any number of dogs and, while not always coming away entirely unscathed, they weren't to be deterred. They had their reputation to maintain. A really juicy story about a Shadow Minister who was into rent-boys would do them no end of good.

Before ringing the doorbell they turned to survey the

garden with its trees and shrubberies and beds of old roses. They were particularly impressed by a large oak tree which Cassidy would presently attempt to climb. It was the perfect setting for a high-class sexual scandal involving an important politician. For one brief moment, as the door began to open and they turned exuding false charm and bonhomie, they glimpsed Mrs Rottecombe's unsmiling face. A second later two heavy white objects hurtled towards them. Wilfred leapt at Butcher Cassidy's throat and fortunately missed. Pickles on the other hand went for a softer target and sank her teeth into Flashgun's thigh. In the ensuing rout the oak tree took on a new attraction. With Wilfred hard on his heels Butcher raced for that tree and managed to grab the lowest branch before Wilfred took a firm grip on his left ankle and locked his jaw. Flashgun, on the other hand, hampered by Pickles's attachment to his left thigh, had tried to get away through the rose bed. It was not the wisest route to take. By the time he reached the other side his hands were torn almost as badly as his leg was bitten and he was yelling for help. His yells were largely drowned by the Butcher's screams. At 70 pounds Wilfred was a heavy dog and given to shaking things he had locked on to.

As the screams continued – they could be heard in Meldrum Slocum – Mrs Rottecombe acted. She got into the reporters' car, drove it out into the road and shut and locked the gate before sauntering back to the scene of such satisfactory carnage. By that time the Postmaster in Little Meldrum had phoned for an ambulance. It was

clearly needed urgently if lives were to be saved. The
Flashgun Kid shared the Postmaster's opinion. Having
dragged Pickles, still firmly attached to his thigh and, by
the feel of things seemingly a permanent fixture, through
the rose bed, he had tripped at the lawn's edge and was
being dragged back the way he'd come through those
same roses. They were old roses on *canina* stock and
exceedingly thorny. They had also been recently mulched
with horse manure. Flashgun made the mistake of
grabbing at them again and this time there could be no
mistaking in Meldrum Slocum the imminence of death at
Leyline Lodge. Butcher Cassidy shared that opinion. He
clung to the branch of the oak with even more
determination than he had pestered the mother, several
mothers in fact, whose daughters had just been
murdered, to find out how they were feeling about the
deaths. Nothing on God's earth was going to make him
let go. Wilfred was obviously of the same opinion. He'd
got that ankle and he meant to keep it. He shook
Butcher's leg, he worried it, he sank his teeth even deeper
into it and took not a blind bit of notice of the suede shoe
on Butcher's other foot that kept kicking him on the side
of the head. Wilfred rather liked being kicked so gently.
Mr Rottecombe had once in a moment of intense
irritation kicked him a damned sight harder and Wilfred
hadn't minded that either. Butcher's kicks merely tickled
him.

Having provided evidence that the reporters had
trespassed by climbing over the locked gate, Mrs

Rottecombe returned from the road. Even she could see it was time to call the bull terriers off before Wilfred removed Butcher Cassidy's foot or the other wretch was savaged to death on the ground.

'That's enough of that,' she commanded, hurrying across to the oak. Wilfred ignored her. He was enjoying that ankle too much. Mrs Rottecombe resorted to sterner measures. She knew her bull terriers. There was no point in clobbering them over the head; the backside was far more vulnerable and in Wilfred's case more accessible. Seizing the dog's scrotum with both hands she applied the nutcracker method with the utmost force. For a moment Wilfred merely grunted but the pain was too much even for him. He opened his mouth to voice a proper protest and was promptly dragged to the ground.

'Naughty dog, naughty dog,' Mrs Rottecombe scolded him. 'You are a very naughty doggie.'

To Butcher, now on top of the branch and scrambling on to an even higher one, there was something insane about those words. Naughty that fucking dog wasn't. It was a canine crocodile, a four-legged mantrap, and he was going to see the brute was put down fast and, he hoped, painfully.

Mrs Rottecombe turned her attention to Pickles who, being a bitch, lacked a scrotum. Instead she seized the nearest weapon, a plant label which announced that the roses were Crimson Glory. Carefully wiping the horse manure and earth off the plastic (she didn't want dear little Pickles to get tetanus or any more terminal lockjaw than she was already displaying), she lifted the bull terrier's tail and jabbed. If anything, Pickles's reaction was more immediate than that of Wilfred. She let go of the Flashgun Kid and shot across the rose bed into the deepest shrubbery to lick her wound. Mrs Rottecombe replaced the metal label and turned her attention to the savaged cameraman.

'What do you think you're doing here?' she demanded with a haughty lack of concern for his injuries that would have taken Flashgun's breath away if he had had any to spare. Flashgun didn't think, he knew what he was doing there. Dying. He looked up at the ghastly woman and managed to speak.

'Help me, help me,' he whimpered. 'I'm bleeding to death.'

'Nonsense,' said Mrs Rottecombe. 'You're trespassing. If you choose to trespass on private property, it's your own fault if you get bitten. There's a sign by the gate. It says quite clearly "BEWARE OF THE DOG". You must have seen it. You ignored it and trespassed and attacked a perfectly harmless family pet and then you are surprised when it defends itself. You are a criminal. And what is that other fellow doing up in my tree?'

Jones's eyes rolled in his head. A woman who could call the murderous brute which had been on the point of gnawing his leg off 'a harmless family pet' had to be clean off her fucking head.

'For Christ's sake . . .' he began but Mrs Rottecombe brushed his prayer aside.

'Name and address,' she snapped. 'Both your names and addresses.' Then realising she was still in her dressing gown, she turned towards the house. 'And just you wait where you are,' she said as she went. 'I intend to call the police and have you both prosecuted for trespass and cruelty to animals.'

The threat was too much for Flashgun. He sank back on to the horse manure and passed out. It was left to Butcher Cassidy, now three branches further up the tree, to protest.

'Cruelty to animals, you fucking bitch,' he shouted at her as she led the chastened Wilfred into the house. 'You're the one who's going to be done for cruelty. We'll fucking crucify you. You see if we don't. We'll sue you for everything you've got.'

Mrs Rottecombe smiled and patted Wilfred. 'Good dog, Wilfie. You're a good dog, aren't you? Nasty man kicked you, didn't he?'

She went into the house and fetched a tube of tomato purée from the kitchen. Holding him by the collar she poured the stuff on to his back. Then she led him out into the garden again and left him underneath the oak tree. He was still there when the ambulance came and shortly afterwards the police. There was blood from Butch's ankle all over the ground under the tree and quite a lot on Wilfred's back where it added authenticity to the tomato purée. Mrs Rottecombe had achieved her object. In an emergency she was a resourceful woman.

14

The Shadow Minister for Social Enhancement sat in the grass against the wall with his head in his hands. He knew now he should never have come home a day early. He was equally certain about his marriage. He should never have come within a mile of the damned woman who could let loose those terrible dogs on two reporters. The sounds of snarls and screams, not to mention the knowledge that there was an unconscious man, his head covered in blood, lying on the floor of the garage convinced him of that. Harold Rottecombe had no intention of being an accessory after the fact of the poor devil being there and possibly even of his murder. If that lot hit the headlines, as it was almost bound to now, his position not only as Shadow Minister but also as an MP would be ended. And it was all the fault of that insane bitch. He should never have married her. A new thought struck him. There had been something genuine about her horror when she'd returned from the garage which almost convinced him she hadn't put him there. Cut that 'almost'. She really hadn't known he was in there. In that case someone else was responsible. Harold Rottecombe searched for another explanation and found one. Someone was out to ruin his career. That was why the newspapers had been informed. Anyway it was too late to do anything about that now. The first thing he had to do was to get back to London by train. There was no way he could drive. A glance over the wall showed him the group of journalists and the TV men down at the bottom of the drive. They would be there all day and the police from Oston would undoubtedly come to the house. He couldn't use the train station there. He'd have to get to Slawford to catch the train to Bristol and London. The town was outside his constituency and he'd be less likely to be recognised there. Against that it was a hell of a long way to have to walk.

On the other hand there was the river. It flowed through Slawford, and along the wall he could see the roof of the boat-house and a far better method than trudging for ten miles across fields occurred to him. He'd take the rowing boat and go downstream.

Behind him Ruth was putting her skills in tying people up to good use on Wilt. Having made sure he wasn't dead or dying she had bound his wrists together with several turns of Elastoplast which wouldn't leave any obvious marks like rope, and removed his jeans. Then she dragged him over to the Volvo estate, in the process getting some of Wilt's own blood on to the Y-fronts, and by using two planks rolled him with great difficulty into the back. Next she tied a handkerchief across his mouth so he could still breathe, and covered him with newspapers and several cardboard boxes. Finally she took his knapsack and jeans, locked the garage doors and returned to the house to wait for Harold to return.

After half an hour she called his name but there was no reply. She went out into the garden and looked over the wall. There was a patch of crushed long grass where he must have sat but no sign of him. He had evidently taken fright and scurried away. It was just as well. She had to deal with the reporters at the gate. They could wait for a bit. She wanted to see what was in the knapsack. She went back to the garage and by the time she'd been through the bag she was completely bewildered. Wilt's driving licence gave his address as 45 Oakhurst Avenue, Ipford. Ipford? But Ipford was away to the south. How come the wretched man had ended up in her garage? Like everything else it made no sense. On the other hand, if she dumped him somewhere near Ipford he'd have a job explaining what he had been doing without his trousers in a sleepy place like Meldrum Slocum. For ten long minutes Mrs Rottecombe sat and considered the problem before making her decision.

An hour later she went down the drive with Wilfred and Pickles and showed the group of media people there the supposed wounds the brutes from the *News on Sunday* had inflicted on Wilfred.

'They trespassed on private property and tried to break into the house and then when Pickles caught them they were foolish enough to kick her. You can't do that to an English bull terrier and not expect the little darling to defend herself, can you, sweetie?' Pickles wagged her tail and looked pleased with herself. She liked being petted. Wilfred was far too heavy to pick up but his hindquarters were impressively swathed in bandages. 'One of the men attacked him with a knife,' she explained. 'That was a really horrid thing to do.'

'No, I'm not prepared to answer any questions,' she said when one reporter began to ask if it was true that— 'I am far too upset. I can't bear cruelty to animals and what those two men did was quite dreadful. No, my husband is in London. If you want to talk to him, you'll find him there. I'm going to get some rest. It's been a very distressing day. I'm sure you can see that.'

What the reporters could see was that Butcher Cassidy and the Flashgun Kid must have been completely insane to go anywhere near such fearsome dogs, and as for kicking the bitch . . . well, they must have been bent on suicide with that enormous Wilfred around. As Mrs Rottecombe went back to the house, opinion was divided among the men at the gate. Some were delighted that Butcher and Flashgun had finally met their match while others seemed to think they had shown immense courage, courage far beyond the call of duty, in pursuit of a story. No one was prepared to follow their example and presently the convoy moved off.

Mrs Rottecombe watched them go and then went back to the house to attend to Wilt.

She put his boots, socks and trousers into a garbage bag. She would dump them somewhere along the way. For a moment she considered taking Wilfred and Pickles but decided against it. She needed to be totally anonymous and people might remember seeing the dogs in the car. Then she checked the bottom of the drive from a bedroom window and was relieved to see that the reporters had left. At 9 p.m. she drove down to the road and was on her way south towards Ipford.

15

Being up at the cabin overlooking Lake Sassaquassee with the quads wasn't making Uncle Wally feel even slightly safer. Not that it was a cabin. As Sheriff Stallard had said Wally Immelmann had built himself an ante-bellum mansion there and had felled nearly ever tree for half a mile around the place because Auntie Joan was frightened of bears and wasn't going to go walking in the woods where she couldn't see if there were bears about. And beyond the open space she'd insisted on his erecting an extremely strong wire fence to make sure as hell bears didn't get in and start marauding around the house and coming through the picture windows that looked out over the terrace and the swimming-pool (she wasn't swimming in the lake because she'd heard there were snakes that swam too, water moccasins and cotton-mouths) and the barbecue area and all. It was the 'all' that excited the Wilt girls. And had always excited Wally which is why he had taken such pains and paid so much to collect it.

'That there is a Sherman tank. Went right through the Second World War,' he told them proudly. 'Up Omaha Beach on D-Day with General Patton – they say he rode into battle on it – and on all the way to Berlin. Well, not right to Berlin because that General Montgomery chickened out taking the city but it got pretty damn close. Best battle tank there was. Now over here is a Huey 'copter with a Puff the Magic Dragon in the door. Knocked the sh . . . knocked the charlies out in 'Nam like they didn't know what hit them. That gun could fire thousands of rounds in no time at all. And this here is a howitzer that was with General MacArthur in Korea and when that baby fired, those yellow-bellies knew that Uncle Sam meant business. Same with this baby.' He indicated a flame-thrower. 'Went in on Okinawa barbecuing Nips like—'

'Barbecuing whats?' Emmeline asked.

'Japs,' said Uncle Wally proudly. 'Shoots flame out the nozzle here and zaps a guy and you got a turkey roast up and running on the hoof. Those bastards were torched in their hundreds. And this here is a napalm bomb. You know what napalm is. It's great stuff. Like cooking oil and jello. You want a village fry-up all you need do is drop one of those and – boom! – you've got a charlie roasted better than anything you've ever seen. Now this is a missile I got from Germany when we won the Cold War. Put a nuclear warhead on that sweetheart and a town five times the size of Wilma you wouldn't even find on a map it would go so fast. The Russkies knew that, which is how we saved the world from Communism. They weren't going to risk nuclear annihilation, no way.'

All over the grounds there were the mementoes of terrible wars but the pride of Uncle Wally's military collection was a B-52. It stood on the other side of the house where it could be seen through the picture window even at night with lights set in the ground shining up on it, a black monstrous bomber with fifty-eight missions over Vietnam and Iraq painted in symbols on the side; it was, as Wally said, capable of flying twelve thousand miles and dropping an H-bomb that would take out the biggest city in the world.

'What does "take out" mean, Uncle Wally?' Josephine asked with seeming innocence. But Wally Immelmann was too immersed in his dream of a world made safe by mass destruction to notice.

'It means first you get the blast wave and second the fireball and third you get radiation and fifteen, sixteen million people dead. That's what it means, honey. Used to keep them flying round the clock, the Strategic Air Force, and all ready to go if the President of the US of A pressed the button. Course we got better weapons now but in their day that baby ruled the sky. And the world. We don't need anything that big now. Got ICBMs and Stealth bombers and Cruise missiles and neutron bombs and stuff no one knows about that can cross the Atlantic like in less than an hour. Best of all there's lasers in outer space that can fry anywhere on earth at the speed of light.'

By the time they got back to the house Uncle Wally was in a genial and generous mood.

'Those girls of yours are smart, real smart,' he told Eva who had been watching rather nervously from a distance.

'I've been giving them a history lesson why we win wars and nobody can get near us technologywise. Isn't that so, girls?'

'Yes, Uncle Wally,' said the quads in unison. Eva looked at them suspiciously. She knew that unison. It was a portent.

That night while Uncle Wally was watching baseball and having his fifth bourbon on the rocks, and Eva and Auntie Joan were talking family back in England, Samantha found an old portable tape recorder in Wally's romper room. It was a reel-to-reel one with an automatic cut-out when the tape came to the end and it had a four-hour reel on it. By the time Wally and his wife staggered up to the bedroom it was running under the doublewide. And Wally wanted a hump.

'Aw, come on, honey pie,' he said. 'We aren't getting any younger and—'

'Speak for yourself,' said Auntie Joan. She wasn't in a good mood. Eva had told her that Maude, who was Auntie Joan's sister, had decided to become a lesbian and was living with a gay who'd had a sex-change operation. That wasn't the sort of family news she wanted. Wally humping her wasn't what she wanted either. Could be something to be said for becoming a lesbian.

'I am speaking for myself,' Wally said. 'Only person I can speak for. You don't have a goddam prostate or if you do I haven't heard that Dr Hellster I go to in Atlanta speak about it. He tells me I got to keep it up or else.'

'Keep it up? You haven't got it to keep up. Leastways

I haven't noticed it lately. You sure you haven't left it in the bathroom along with your hairpiece? Like trying to get some action out of a sea slug.'

'Yeah,' said Wally, evidently ignoring the comparison with difficulty. 'And I'm not likely to get it up if you don't give me some foreplay.'

'Foreplay? You think a woman's got to do the foreplay? You've got the wrong woman if you think that. You're the one supposed to do the foreplay. Like with the tongue and all.'

'Sweet fuck!' said Uncle Wally. 'At your age you want me playing the old mouth-organ? Like whale blowing in reverse? Shit. This is no time to be making cracks like that.'

'Well, it isn't the time to be asking me to go down on you either.'

'I wasn't talking about going down. Last time you did that must have been around the time of the Watergate hearings.'

'Tasted like it too,' said Auntie Joan. After more argument she agreed to lie back and pretend Wally was Arnold Schwarzenegger on barbiturates, something that slowed him up.

'Only thing slowing me up is finding the thing,' said Wally. 'Like going down Oak Creek Canyon on a wet night and no flashlight. You sure you still got a pussy? That surgeon didn't do a total when you had that hysterectomy?'

In the end he found what he had been looking for. Or thought he had. Auntie Joan put him right.

'Asshole!' she shrieked. 'Jesus, are you insane trying to brown-ass me? Oh no, you don't, Wally Immelmann. I'm fucked if you're going to sodomise me. You want to do that with someone, find yourself a guy who likes it that way. I sure as shit don't.'

'Sodomise? I wasn't trying to sodomise you,' said Wally, genuinely outraged. 'We been married all these years, thirty years, thirty goddam years, I ever tried to sodomise you?'

'Yes,' said Auntie Joan bitterly. 'Yes, you have and don't I know it. Dr Cohen says it's—'

'Dr Cohen? You been telling Dr Cohen I've been sodomising you? I'm not hearing this. I can't be!' Wally yelled. 'Telling Dr Cohen . . . Jesus.'

'I didn't need to tell him. He's got eyes in his head. He could see for himself and he was disgusted. He says it's against the law. And he's right.'

Wally was no longer interested in humping. He was sitting bolt upright in the doublewide.

'Against the law? That's bullshit. If it's against the law how come gays are doing it all the time and we got an epidemic of Aids?'

'Not that law. The Law of God. Dr Cohen says it's there in the Bible. "Thou shalt not—"'

'The Bible? What's Dr Cohen know about the Bible? That New Jersey kike think the Jews wrote the Bible, for Chrissake? He's got to be crazy.'

'Wally dear, who else?' said Auntie Joan, seizing the initiative now that Wally was off her and into a morass of ignorance. 'Who else wrote the Bible?'

'What you mean, who else? Genesis did, and Joshua and Jonah. Guys like that. That's who wrote the Bible.'

'You're forgetting Moses,' said Auntie Joan smugly. 'Like in Dr Moses Cohen. Jews, Wally dear. Jews. The Bible was written by Jews. Hadn't you noticed?'

'Jesus,' said Wally Immelmann.

'Him too. Matthew, Mark, Luke and John. All Jews, Wally, and that's the gospel.'

Wally slumped down on to the bed. 'Sure, sure I know all that,' he said with a whimper. 'And you have to go and tell Dr Cohen I make a habit of sodomising you. You've got to be crazy and I mean out of your head altogether. Clinically.'

'I tell you I didn't tell him. He could see for himself when I went for my cervical and he was disgusted. You should have heard what he said about men who did that sort of thing. Had me take a blood test.'

'Don't tell me!' yelled Wally and of course she did. At length and in the most explicit detail while he kept interrupting her with threats of what he was going to do to her. Like divorce her and he knew some guys who would fix her for good.

'Big deal!' Auntie Joan shouted back. 'You think I haven't got myself insurance? Dr Cohen gave me the name of a lawyer, a real good one, and I've seen him. You make one move against me, Wally Immelmann, and you're going to see what dope I've sworn on you. You wouldn't believe it.'

Wally said he couldn't believe a wife would do a thing like that, betraying her husband to a fucking doctor and a lawyer. They continued shouting until he was exhausted and lay back in bed wondering what he was going to do. One thing was certain. He was going to have to change his doctor and go to Dr Lesky. It was the last thing he wanted to do. Dr Lesky believed in abortion. It wouldn't look good going to a doctor like Dr Lesky and being the Deacon of the Church of the Living Lord. Living Lorders didn't go to abortionists and he wasn't going to that clinic for blacks and down-and-outs. You got more diseases there than cures. Even the doctors contracted them. Like Immelmann Enterprises going on welfare. Wally lay in the darkness and tried to think how to get round Dr Cohen. Being a Deacon and having it thought he was a sodomist wasn't going to do him any good in Wilma at all.

What the Drug Enforcement Agents had been installing in the Starfighter Mansion wasn't going him any good either.

'We've put double bugs in every room and that way when he scans he finds one but he misses the other. That's only activated when we want it on so the scanner won't pick it up first time. He won't scan twice because he'll have found the first one and they never check again,' the electronic device expert told the meeting. 'And the way we know when to turn the number 2s on is we've got video cameras so small they make a fly's eye look big. No way you can spot them. They show us who's there and the audios pick up every word. If this guy is running any racket we'll get the proof. The only way he can talk in private is outside in the open air and even then he can't be too sure. Could be behind a shirt button, any place. So we've got his vehicular transportation all tapped and his house so tight we can tell if he washes behind his ears or been circumcised. Only thing puzzling me is why we're going to all this trouble with this guy. I mean, this is Mafia equipment we've installed and this has got to be small beer.'

'Could be very big,' Palowski said. 'Our information from Poland is that this stuff is a new super high-grade designer from a Russian laboratory. No need to grow it and it's a thousand times more addictive than crack. Street value into gigabucks and as easy to make as speed. Easier. Which could explain why Sol is missing. Lose a sample like that and you lose your life. Which is almost certainly what's happened to him. Now, Sheriff Stallard says Immelmann Enterprises is diversifying into pharmaceuticals. That's the rumour he's heard. Some German firm is interested in investing with him and they've been investing in Russia too. That's why the interest in Washington. My guess is this could be a subversion gambit. Militarily the Russians are out of the game but if they can infiltrate a designer drug of this calibre they don't need a war to win.'

'That guy is paranoid, I swear to God. He's got Russkies on the brain,' the electronics expert said afterwards.

It was an opinion shared by Sheriff Stallard when Baxter reported that the Starfighter Mansion had been wired for S & S like sight and sound.

'You mean when Wally Immelmann . . . when Mrs Immelmann goes to the bathroom some guy's going to be filming her on the can? I don't believe it. And I sure as hell don't want to see any footage of her taking a slash.'

'It gets worse . . .'

'Worse? Nothing could be worse than Joanie . . . Where's the fucking camera? And don't tell me they're shooting from below. I'll throw up.'

'No, it's a straight angle,' said Baxter. 'But they can zoom in. I mean, Sheriff, they're using space technology in there.'

'You can say that again,' said the Sheriff, still obsessed with the thought of Auntie Joan on the toilet. 'What do they think there is to zoom in on? Those guys some sort of perverts? I mean, they've got to be. They'll be breaking every obscenity regulation there is. And what the hell do they want filming in there?'

'Just in case Wally tries to flush the stuff down. They want a record of it. And that's another thing. They've brought in the Shit Squad.'

'You've told me,' said the Sheriff. 'Pretty apt damned name for the bastards. I couldn't put it better myself.'

'No, these guys are different.'

'I'll say they are. The same as me they're not. I don't get any kicks out of spying on fat women pissing in the privacy of their own bathrooms. You've got to be a genuine pervert to like that.'

'No, the Shit Squad are sewage experts. They've hooked into all the effluent coming out of the Starfighter and are running it into a tanker for analysis. The thing is parked round the back of the old drive-in movie screen and it's enormous. Must take fifteen thousand gallons a throw. And the lab truck is there too where it can't be seen. They've got equipment in there that can trace drugs in athletes' urine weeks after they've taken them.'

Sheriff Stallard was gaping at him. Nothing in a long career as a Law Enforcement Officer came anywhere like this. 'They've hooked . . .? Say it again, Baxter, say it again and slowly this time. This stuff is not getting through to me.'

'It's like this,' said Baxter. 'They've sealed off all the outlets from the house, all the water and sewage pipes, and they've hooked this huge sucking device on so that they can pump it—'

'Shit,' said the Sheriff. 'These guys are using taxpayers' money to test all the urine comes out of Wally Immelmann's place? You'll be telling me next they've got this satellite in statutory orbit over Wilma.' He stopped and looked in horror up into the sky. 'Could be reading the letters on my badge.'

'I think the word is "stationary". Stationary orbit. You said "statutory orbit".'

Sheriff Stallard turned his glazed eyes on his Deputy. He was beginning to feel quite mad. 'Stationary, Baxter, stationary it can't be. Wilma's moving at around three thousand miles an hour. Has to be because that's the speed the world goes round. Something like that. You can work it out. The world goes round once a day and the circumference is twenty-four thousand miles. So twenty-four goes into twenty-four thousand a thousand times. Work it out yourself. Well, if you've got a satellite out there squatting over Wilma . . . no, not squatting, let's cut the squatting. I don't want to think about that again. It's up there even further out than Wilma, and Wilma's way out enough for me the way those guys are acting, that baby has to be moving even faster just to keep up. Right?' Baxter nodded. 'Good. So when I said "statutory" I mean "statutory". This operation has to be costing millions. So it's got to be statutory. Washington's approval. And who's been talking about cutting the Federal deficit?'

He went back to his office and took a Tylenol and lay down and tried to pretend nothing was happening. He couldn't. The image of Joanie Immelmann on the can overwhelmed him.

In Oston Police Station Bob Battleby continued to protest his innocence. He hadn't set fire to his own house. Why would he do a thing like that? It was a beautiful house and his family had owned it for hundreds of years. He was very fond of it and so on. As for porno mags and the other stuff, he had no idea how they had got into his Range Rover. Perhaps the firemen had put them there. It was the sort of muck people like firemen tended to read. No, he didn't know any firemen personally, they weren't the class of people he usually mixed with – but they were never doing anything useful. They hadn't saved his house from being burnt to the ground, for instance, and reading porn, he supposed, helped them to pass the time. The handcuffs and the gag and whips? Did he really imagine the firemen made use of them, too, to pass the time? Well no, now that he came to think about it he didn't suppose they did. They sounded more like things the police might have a use for.

That comment didn't go down at all well with the Inspector putting the questions in the absence of the Superintendent who was catching up on his sleep. Battleby wasn't so fortunate. The questions kept on coming and he wasn't going to get any sleep until he answered them correctly. Where was his wife? He didn't have one. Was he on good terms with his family? They could mind their own fucking business. But that was exactly what they were doing; their business was arresting criminals and, for his information, men who set fire to their own houses and possessed Obscene Material of a paedophile nature, not to mention punching Superintendents in the face, came into the category, several categories of criminals.

Battleby said he hadn't set fire to his own house. Mrs Rottecombe could prove that. She'd been with him when he left the kitchen. The Inspector raised his eyebrows. But Mrs Rottecombe had made a sworn statement that she'd been waiting for him in her car outside the front door. Battleby made an even fouler sworn statement about Mrs fucking Rottecombe, and merely pointed out that as the Arson Squad had begun their investigations and were being helped by the Insurance Company investigators who were the real experts, they would soon know. What the Inspector would like to know was the state of Battleby's finances. Battleby refused to answer. It didn't matter, they'd get a court order to see his bank accounts. It was normal procedure in cases of arson where so much insurance money was involved. He had insured it, of course? Battleby supposed so. He left money matters to his accountant. But the house was insured in his name? Of course it bloody was. Had to be. After all, his family had lived in it for two hundred and more years so it had to be in his name. Quite so. Now, about the Obscene Material . . . Mrs Rottecombe had made a statement saying he had asked her to tie him up and whip him and she'd refused . . . Like hell she had. The bloody bitch enjoyed whipping and torturing people. She was into fladge in a big way . . . He stopped. Even in his state of almost total fatigue he could see from the Inspector's expression that he'd said the wrong thing. He asked to speak to his solicitor. Of course he could. Just give them the number and the lawyer's name and he could phone him. Battleby couldn't remember his solicitor's telephone number. The man was up in London and . . . Would he like a local solicitor? No, he fucking wouldn't. The only thing those dunderheads knew about was boundary disputes.

And so the questioning had gone on and on and every

time Battleby's head drooped on to the table he was shaken awake. He was even given strong coffee and allowed to use the toilet. Then the questions began again. A different officer took over at midday and put the same questions.

16

At Ipford Police Station, Inspector Flint shared the Sheriff's feeling about Drug Enforcement Agents. He had just read Superintendent Hodge's report on Mrs Wilt and was appalled.

'You can't send this stuff across to America,' he protested. 'There wasn't a shred of evidence the Wilts had anything to do with the distribution of drugs in Ipford. They were as clean as a whistle.'

'Only because someone blew one for them,' said Hodge.

'Meaning?' said Flint whose blood pressure had soared. 'Meaning?'

'Meaning they were tipped off we were on to them and they took cover in the American airbase and dumped the stuff.'

'I hope you're not suggesting I had anything to do—'

'Not you, Flint. Just take a dekko at the evidence. Wilt has this job teaching Yanks at Lakenheath and this guy Immelmann's been stationed there. So Wilt's got contacts with Yanks even before he starts. That's one. Two is PCP is an American drug. Designer drug and the Lord Lieutenant's daughter dies of an overdose at the Tech where Wilt teaches her. ODs on PCP. There's more evidence, a whole heap of it and it all points one way. To the Wilts. You can't deny it, Flint. And another thing. Where else was Wilt teaching? In the hoosegow here in Ipford.'

'Hodge, we don't have hoosegows in Britain. You've got America on the brain.'

'All right. Wilt was teaching in the prison and mixing with some of the nastiest villains in the drug business. That's three strikes against the bastard. Number four is—'

'Hodge, don't let me interrupt you but you can't have four strikes in baseball. Miss three and you're out. If you really want to go transatlantic, you've got to get these things right. You'll never make the Yankee Stadium if you go on like this.'

'Very funny, I'm sure. You always were known for your wit. Well, this time just stick to the evidence. Mrs Wilt's aunt is married to a known drug importer in the States. OK, they're legit those drugs. On the surface. Then again he's got a place in the Caribbean and a motor boat that does over sixty knots and on top of that he has planes. Learjets and Beechcraft. All the apparatus for a highly lucrative drug pusher. And Mrs Wilt just happens to visit him with her quads. Very good diversionary tactics those quads. And to top it all Wilt isn't home and no one knows where he's hidden himself. It adds up, it all adds up. You've got to admit that.'

Flint hitched his chair forward. 'Wilt's hidden himself? No one knows where he's got to? Are you certain about that?' he asked.

Hodge nodded triumphantly. 'Add this to the catalogue,' he said. 'The day Mrs Wilt flies into Atlanta her husband goes to the building society and draws out a large sum in cash. In cash. And where does he leave his credit cards and passport? At home. On the kitchen table. That's right, on the kitchen table,' he said as Flint's face registered astonishment. 'Bed not made. Washing-up not done. Dirty plates still on the table. Drawers in the chest of drawers in the bedroom open. Car still in the garage. Nothing missing except Mr Henry Wilt. Not a bloody thing. Even his shoes are there. We got the cleaning lady to check them out. So what does that tell you?'

'It makes a change,' said Flint sourly. He disliked being wrong-footed, especially by clowns like Hodge.

'Makes a change? What's that supposed to mean?' Hodge demanded.

'It means just this. The first time I ran into Wilty, it was his wife was missing. Supposed to be down a damned great pile hole at the Tech. Only it just so happens Wilt has stuffed an inflatable plastic doll dressed in Mrs Eva bloody Wilt's clothes down there and they put twenty tons of pre-mix on top of her. In fact she is living it up with a couple of daffy Americans on a stolen boat on the Broads. So where is Mrs Wilt now? Sitting pretty . . . well, as near pretty as she'll ever get at any rate, in the United States and it's our Henry who is missing. Yes, that makes a change. It does indeed.'

'You don't think he's done a runner?' Hodge asked.

'With Wilt I've given up thinking. I have not the

faintest idea what goes on in that mad blighter's mind. All I do know is it won't be what you think it is. It's going to be something you wouldn't even dream of thinking about. So don't ask me what he's done. I wouldn't have a clue.'

'Well, my guess is he's getting himself an alibi,' said Hodge.

'With his credit cards and all on the kitchen table?' said Flint. 'And none of his clothes missing? Doesn't sound much like a voluntary disappearance to me. Sounds more like something has happened to the little bastard. Have you checked the hospital?'

'Of course I have. The first thing I did. Checked every goddam hospital in the area. No one answering his description has been booked in. I've checked the morgues, the lot, and he is not around. Makes you think, doesn't it?'

'No,' said Flint firmly. 'It does not. I've told you. Where Henry Wilt is concerned I don't even try to think. It hurts too much.'

All the same when Superintendent Hodge left Flint sat on considering the situation.

'There isn't a snowball's chance in hell of Wilty being involved in drugs,' he told Sergeant Yates. 'And can you see Eva Wilt in what that madman Hodge would call that "ball game"? I'm damned if I can. They may be crazy, the Wilts, but they're the least likely people to start committing real crimes.'

'I know, sir,' said Yates. 'But Hodge is presenting a

pretty nasty profile to the American authorities. I mean, it doesn't look good all that stuff about Lakenheath and so on.'

'It's all purely circumstantial. He hasn't got even the tiniest shred of real evidence,' said Flint. 'Let's just hope the police over there see that. I wouldn't want the Wilt family up before an American court. Not after the OJ trial. Television in the courtroom and everyone becomes a bloody actor. And we know what twerps they are.' He paused in thought. 'I wonder where the hell our Henry's got to, though. That's the real mystery.'

17

'I'm so worried about Henry,' Eva told Auntie Joan. 'I've tried calling him time and again – seven times today – and he's never in.'

'Maybe he's teaching this course you told me about. The one about Tradition and Culture for Canadians.'

'But that only takes up an hour or two and he wouldn't be teaching it at six in the morning,' said Eva. 'I mean, the time difference is five hours, isn't it?'

'It's five hours later in the UK. The time there now must be around midnight,' said Auntie Joan. In his chair in front of the TV Uncle Wally groaned. He'd had a hard day trying to keep the thought of Dr Cohen and the scandal of being known as a sodomiser out of his mind. It was impossible. Life in Wilma could become impossible. The scandal had come at the worst possible time just when he was thinking of diversifying Immelmann Enterprises into pharmaceuticals. And here he was saddled with a woman who didn't know that English time was five hours ahead of Eastern US time. Like she didn't understand the sun rose in the east.

'But then he must be at home,' said Eva, her anxiety reaching a new pitch. 'I've been phoning him every day around this time because he finishes his course by midday and he never stays out late at night. Do you think I should try again?'

'Yes,' said Wally. 'I definitely think you should. He could have had an accident. Guy down in Alabama fell off a stepladder last fall and his wife kept calling and he couldn't reach the phone. Couldn't make the fridge either. Died of starvation. That and thirst. They didn't find him until some kids broke in and there he was nothing but skin and bone.'

He didn't have to say any more. Eva was already in the bedroom trying to get through again.

'You didn't have to tell her that,' said Auntie Joan. 'That was a real mean thing to say.'

'I did and it wasn't. Like being cooped up in prison with her and those nieces of yours.'

'And yours, Wally Immelmann, your nieces too.'

Wally smiled a nasty smile and shook his head. 'I married you, honey, not your fucking family. Ain't no blood relations of mine.'

Before another full-scale quarrel could develop Eva had returned with the news that the phone at home had rung and rung and Henry still hadn't answered.

'Guy's got good sense not to,' said Wally to himself. He didn't say it out loud.

'Isn't there some friend you could get to see where he is?' Auntie Joan asked.

Eva said Henry didn't like the Mottrams and he wasn't on good terms with the neighbours.

'His best friend is Peter Braintree. I suppose I could try them.'

She went back into the bedroom and came out five minutes later.

'They don't answer either,' she said. 'It's the summer holidays and they always go away.'

'Perhaps Henry has gone with them,' said Auntie Joan.

But Eva wasn't convinced. 'He'd have told me if he'd been going to do that. He definitely said he had to stay behind because he has this course for the Canadians to teach. We need the money for the girls' education.'

'From what they said to the Revd Cooper . . .' Wally began and was silenced by a look from his wife.

'Tomorrow we'll go out in the sail boat and have ourselves a picnic,' she said. 'It's really nice out on the lake this time of the year.'

In the swimming-pool the quads were having a wonderful time.

'Honestly, how those girls do enjoy the pool,' said Auntie Joan. 'They're having a whale of a time.'

'Sure are,' said Uncle Wally. He reckoned he knew why they were so peculiar. With a mother as dumb as Eva it was surprising they could talk. For the first time he was surprised to find himself feeling fond of them. They took his mind off his other worries.

But Eva's thoughts were concentrated on Henry. It wasn't like him to be out all the time. And he couldn't have gone away. If he had, he would certainly have phoned to let her know. She didn't know who to turn to.

Besides, if anything had happened to him like he'd been knocked over or been taken ill, someone would have got in touch with her. She'd left her name and Auntie Joan's address and telephone number on the cork pin board in the kitchen where no one could miss it and just to be on the safe side had given it to Mavis Mottram. Henry might not like Mavis or Patrick Mottram and they certainly didn't like him – Mavis's feelings amounted to loathing because, Eva suspected, she'd once made a pass at Henry and he'd told her where to get off – but even so Mavis would have been the first to let her know if anything serious had happened. She'd relish doing it. On the other hand Eva didn't relish having to phone Mavis and ask her what Henry was doing. She'd only do that as a last resort. In the meantime she tried to console herself with the thought that the girls were learning so much and having such a good time with it.

She was unknowingly correct on both counts. Josephine and Samantha had retrieved the tape recorder from under the bed and on the excuse that they just wanted a quiet day playing music in their room asked could they borrow Uncle Wally's earphones so as not to disturb him and Auntie Joan.

Uncle Wally jumped at the opportunity. 'Make yourselves at home, feel free,' he said enthusiastically, showing them his music workroom. 'I built this sound system myself and though I do say it, it's got to be the best this side of Nashville, Tennessee. Man, I doubt even Elvis himself had anything this powerful. I call it my music operations centre. With the equipment I got in here I can blast a boat out of the water with Tina Turner at three miles. And deafen a fucking . . . well, anyway a bear at five hundred yards. The way I look at it, girls, you got to have decibels, and I'm telling you the speakers I got installed in the grounds up trees and you name it, all water- and weatherproofed, are so powerful I could play a tape of a Shuttle launch and it would make more noise than the real thing. Did it for your auntie because she don't like bears too much so I got this gunfire tape and I put it on a timing device so it goes off every hour we're away. And I can vary it, too. Sometimes only every four hours and then three shots in a few minutes. I got a banshee sound, too, that don't do intruders any good. Come over the gate or the fence and sensors in the ground pick up the intruder and all hell breaks loose. Tried it out one time on a guy who came to serve an injunction on me. He got through the gates OK and then I closed them automatically behind him and let this baby go full bore. Couldn't tell he was screaming till I switched it off. Could see he wasn't having the nicest time because he was trying to climb the gates to get out and running around like he was crazy. He dived in the lake in the end and I had to fish him out because he couldn't swim. Couldn't hear, either, by that time. I never did get that injunction. I reckon he lost it someplace like he lost his hearing for a while. Wanted to sue but didn't get no place. No witness and bears don't give evidence in court and besides, I've got influence in these parts. When I talk people listen to old Wally Immelmann and no mistake. Learn something, too.'

The quads had thanked Uncle Wally and had taken the earphones up to their room and listened to him and Auntie Joan having their spat in bed. And they certainly learnt something, too. So while he was busy playing mechanics with the Sherman turret and keeping his head down, the quads returned to the music operations centre – Auntie Joan and Eva were baking cookies in the kitchen and Eva was saying how difficult Henry had become and how he needed a new job instead of being stuck at that stuffy old Tech – and went quietly about their business. It was not business Auntie Joan or Eva would have liked knowing about and Uncle Wally's feelings would have been inexpressible. They found another long reel tape and made a copy of the one they had already heard. Uncle Wally was most helpful. He was beginning to think the only thing wrong with those girls was that they went to a Godless school run by nuns. What they needed was a good American education and help with acquiring good old American know-how. So he came out of the turret and showed them his equipment again and how to do things with it like with the timer and how to copy from reel to reel, and he was very impressed how quickly they picked it all up.

'Those girls of yours have real talent,' he told Eva when they were having coffee in the kitchen mid-afternoon. 'You should let them come over here for their schooling.

Put them in Wilma High School and they'd be real Americans no time at all.'

Eva was pleased to hear it and said so. Unfortunately Henry was such a stick-in-the-mud he wouldn't ever consider emigrating.

By the evening the quads had got Uncle Wally to set up the music operations centre and the timing device to play when they were all out on the lake having a picnic on the island where Uncle Wally had another barbecue.

'I'd show you what this system can produce in decibels except your auntie doesn't like it real loud,' he said. 'Now what shall we play? Nothing too heavy. Your auntie just loves Abba. I guess it's kind of old-fashioned for you but it's soothing and we'll hear it real good.' He put the reel on the machine and fed the tape through and presently the house was filled with sound. In the kitchen Auntie Joan had to shout to make Eva hear what she was saying.

'I hear that Abba again I'm going to go crazy!' she screamed. 'I keep telling him I don't like it any more but he doesn't listen. Men! I said, "Men!"'

Eva said Henry didn't listen to her either. I mean, if she had told him he needed more ambition once she'd told him a thousand times. Auntie Joan nodded. She hadn't heard a word.

In the music operations centre Uncle Wally turned the tape off and smiled happily. 'Reverses itself automatically,' he told the quads. 'That way you get music non-stop. I tell you one time I had Frankie Sinatra singing

"My Way" up here for a month. Of course I'm not around but they told me you could hear it fifteen miles away no problem and that's with the wind blowing the opposite direction. A guy over Lossville way had to buy a machine-gun to stop the bear stampede from trampling his place to death they were so desperate to get away their way. I've told your auntie she's only got to whistle "My Way" and them bears are going to hit the trail. Won't come nowhere near her. And it's got its own independent power plant. Guys trying to burglarise here can cut the main power line it won't make any difference. Got electricity backup. Now that's what I call American know-how. I bet they don't teach you that in England. And them Roman nuns don't know nothing. Never been . . . well, I guess you girls could benefit from some of that American know-how.'

The quads already had. While he went to watch a movie and drink some whiskey they took the label off the Abba reel, put it on the one they had made and fed it through just like Uncle Wally had shown them. Then they wiped the Abba reel and put it away in a box and went through to be nice to Auntie Joan and have some cookies.

Next day it rained and even Uncle Wally had to agree it was no time for going out for a picnic.

'Best be getting back to Wilma. I got an important meeting tomorrow and this rain's going to stick around.'

They packed into his four-wheeler and drove down the dirt road through the forest. Behind them the timer on the music centre ticked ominously. It was set for six that evening and the volume was at maximum. According to Uncle Wally that was like one thousand decibels.

On the way Eva said she was going to call the neighbours in Oakhurst Avenue even though Henry didn't get along with them.

'He's very private,' she said. 'He hates people to know what he's doing.'

'Makes sense,' said Uncle Wally. 'It's a free country. Everyone's entitled to privacy. That's the First Amendment. No one has to incriminate himself.'

'What's "incriminate" mean, Uncle Wally?' Emmeline asked.

Uncle Wally swelled in the driver's seat. He liked being asked questions. He had all the answers. 'Incriminate oneself means to say things that could damage your reputation or land you in court on a criminal charge. It's like it's three words, "In" and "Crime" and "State". That's the way to remember things. Break them up into little lots.'

From their rented house across the street Palowski and Murphy watched the jeep turn in to the Starfighter Mansion and the gates open automatically.

'Big Foot's back,' Murphy told the Surveillance Truck in the disused drive-in over the scrambler.

'We got him onscreen,' came the reply. 'No problem. Vision sound on.'

Murphy sat back and had to agree that all systems were

working perfectly. The screen in the room showed Auntie Joan getting out of the four-wheeler and going into the house.

'Only problem we've got is that Mrs Immelmann. Need wide screen to get her all in,' he told Palowski. 'That's sumo on steroids. And here comes another bulk carrier.' Eva and the quads had entered the hall. 'I don't want to see either of them undressing. Put you off sex for life.'

Palowski was more interested in the Wilt girls.

'Clever using kids like that. Quads. Like they're special. Nobody's going to suspect they're carriers. That Mrs Wilt can't have any feelings. She gets ten to twenty she's going to lose custody. If I hadn't seen that report from the Brits on her record I wouldn't have thought it possible she'd be involved. Too much to lose.'

'Weightwise she could afford to. But some people never learn and those girls are more than good cover. Gets a good lawyer to plead for her and work up public sympathy it could be she wouldn't do any time. Depends how much they were carrying.'

'Sol said a sample, he thought. She could claim she don't even know it's there.'

'For sure. Not that I care so much about her. It's that Immelmann bastard I'm out to nail. What's the schedule for the other house, the one up by the lake?'

Murphy talked to the Surveillance Centre.

'Says they should have moved in by now. You reckon that place is important?'

'Got its own air strip. Could be the ideal place for a lab to make the shit.'

But Murphy wasn't listening. Auntie Joan had gone to the toilet.

18

Harold Rottecombe reached the boat-house to find the brilliant plan he had devised to save having to cut across the fields to Slawford wasn't going to work. It was clearly out of the question. The river, swollen by the downpour that had driven Wilt to the whisky bottle, swirled past the boat-house in full spate, carrying with it branches of trees, empty plastic bottles, a whole bush that had been swept from the bank, someone's suitcase and, most alarmingly of all, a dead sheep. Harold Rottecombe eyed that sheep for a moment – it passed too quickly for him to dwell on it for long – and instantly came to the conclusion that he had no intention of sharing its fate. The little rowing boat in the boat-house wouldn't drift downstream; it would hurtle and be swamped. There was nothing for it. He would have to walk to Slawford after all. And Slawford was ten miles downriver. It was a long time, a very long time since Harold had walked ten miles. In fact it was quite a long time since he had walked two. Still, there was nothing for it. He wasn't going back to the house to face the media mob. Ruth had got them into this mess and she could get them out of it. He set off along the river bank. The ground was soggy from the torrential rain, his shoes weren't made for trudging through long wet grass and, when he rounded the bend in the river, he found himself confronted by a barbed-wire fence that ran down to the water's edge. It stood in two feet of water where the river had overflowed. Harold looked at the fence and despaired. Even without the rushing water he would not have attempted to climb round it or over it. That way lay castration. But several hundred yards up the fence there was a gate. He headed for it, found it locked and was forced to climb painfully over it. After that he had to make several detours to find gaps or gates in hedges and the gaps were always too narrow for a man of his size to squeeze through while the gates were invariably locked. Then there was the barbed wire. Even the hedges that would have looked attractive on a nice summer day turned out on closer inspection to be festooned with barbed wire. Harold Rottecombe, Member of Parliament for a rural constituency and previously a spokesman for farming interests, came to detest farmers. He'd always despised them as greedy, ill-informed and generally uncouth creatures but never before had he realised the malicious delight they obviously took in preventing innocent walkers from crossing their land. And of course with so many detours to make to find gates or something he could get through, and parts of fields that were flooded, the ten miles he'd dreaded looked like becoming more like thirty.

In fact he never reached Slawford.

As he staggered wearily along he cursed his wife. The stupid bitch had been raving mad to set the dogs on those two bloody reporters from the *News on Sunday* instead of being tactful. He was just considering what he would do to her and coming to the conclusion that short of murder she had him by the short and curlies, when it began to rain again. Harold Rottecombe hurried on and came to a stream which led into the river, and trudged up it looking for a place to cross. Then his sodden left shoe came off. With a curse he sat down on the bank and discovered his sock had a hole in it. Worse still his heel was blistered and there was blood. He took the sock off to have a look and as he did so (he was thinking of tetanus) his shoe rolled down the bank into the water. The stream was flowing fast now but he no longer cared. Without that damned shoe he'd never get to Slawford. In a frantic attempt to get his hands on it before it was swept away he slid down the bank, landed painfully on a sharp stone and a moment later was flat on his face in the water and struggling to get up. As the water carried him down his head hit a branch that hung down over the stream and by the time he reached the river he was only partly conscious and in no condition to deal with the torrent. For a moment his head emerged before being sucked under by the current. Unnoticed, he passed below the stone bridge at Slawford and continued on his way to the Severn and the Bristol Channel. Long before that he had lost more than his political hopes. The late Shadow Minister for Social Enhancement swept on his way towards the sea.

19

Sheriff Stallard and Baxter were on their way too. In the police car on the dirt road that led to Lake Sassaquassee. Alerted by the guy at Lossville, who'd had trouble with the stampeding bears, that Mr and Mrs Immelmann were having a quarrel that had to be heard to be believed and if the police didn't hurry and get there soon someone was going to die, the Sheriff was puzzled. He couldn't see how anyone who admitted he was at home ten miles from the Immelmann place could know what was going on there. By the time he got within five miles he knew exactly. Even with the car windows shut it was possible to hear Auntie Joan yelling that she was fucked if she was going to be sodomised and that if Wally wanted to do that dirty thing with someone he'd better find a gay who enjoyed it. The Sheriff didn't like it either and the man at Lossville said his wife couldn't bear it. Listening to it, that is. He was thinking of suing. He'd had enough trouble shooting all those bears without a licence and they were protected animals and the fucking police . . . The Sheriff turned the communications off. He was more interested in hearing about Dr Cohen and it was coming through loud and clear. At four miles. Not that the Sheriff knew that.

He'd never been up to the Immelmann house before. On the other hand he'd never heard anyone shout that loud even in the next room. The man at Lossville was right. This was a domestic dispute to end all domestic disputes. And the business about the Watergate hearings tasting and where her pussy was and had she been totalled when she'd had the hysterectomy was too incredible to put into words. Leastways not so fucking loud the whole world could hear it.

'How far now?' the Sheriff yelled above the din.

'Got another two miles,' Baxter told him.

The Sheriff looked at him as if he was a crazy. 'What do you mean two miles? Stop the car. They've got to be right here. Somewhere real close.'

Baxter stopped the car and the Sheriff opened the door to get out. He didn't get far. 'Shit!' he screamed, slamming the door shut and putting his hands over his ears. 'Get the hell out of here.'

'What did you say?' Baxter yelled, trying to compete with Auntie Joan and the Book of Genesis being written by a Jew of that name.

'I said, let's get the fuck out of here before we go deaf. And call up the Public Nuisance Services. They've got to have someone who can deal with this. Tell them it's a Number One Emergency Noisewise.'

Baxter swung the car round on the wet dirt and the Sheriff clung to his seat-belt as they slithered near the edge of a long drop. Then they were heading back to Wilma and Baxter was trying to get contact. All he got was a guy at Lossville screaming that he was going out of his mind and why didn't someone do something like bomb the Immelmann fucking house. Something sensible and would his wife please put that gun down because shooting him wasn't going to stop the goddam noise. His wife could be heard saying she was going to shoot herself if those fucking filthy revelations didn't stop.

'Put out a Three AAA all bands!' shouted the Sheriff as the car hurtled down the road.

'A Three AAA?' Baxter yelled back. 'An Atomic Attack Alert? Jesus, we can't do that. We could be starting a fucking World War.'

He tried Emergency Services again and couldn't make himself heard. But by then the domestic dispute was coming to an end. There was a brief moment's respite while the tape rewound and then it started again. Auntie Joan was screaming about sea slugs and Wally leaving his toupee in the bathroom.

Sheriff Stallard couldn't believe it. 'But she's said all that before. Every single word. She's got to be out of her mind.'

'Could be they are on this new drug,' said Baxter. 'I mean, they got to be on some God-awful substance to carry on like this.'

'I wish to God I had some substance to be on!' yelled the Sheriff and pondered the possibility that he already was. It had to be something like that. He'd never experienced a noise of this magnitude in all his career.

*

The same could be said for the Electronic Surveillance Team that had been sent to bug the Bear Fort. They had just begun to climb the wire fence around the perimeter when the clock and the tape timer struck six and simultaneously triggered the sound system and Wally Immelmann's most sophisticated deterrent. The latter was not intended for bears. Wally's enemy this time was burglarisers and he had used American know-how to excellent effect. In fact he had done more. He had devised a means of adding utility to the merely aesthetic and historical interest of his collection of military memorabilia. As the first bugging expert dropped to the ground he set off the sensors and immediately four anti-aircraft searchlights swung round and focused on him. So did the guns in the Sherman and the other armoured vehicles. The agents saw them coming and threw themselves flat as the searchlights swung over them. The man on the far side of the fence didn't. Blinded by the lights and deafened by the sound of Auntie Joan's yelling about not giving Wally any foreplay he stumbled about helplessly and added his screams to the din. Behind the searchlights the engines of the armoured vehicles and the Sherman roared into life and then the whole place lit up and the searchlights went out. By the time he could see (he still couldn't hear) he was aware of the Sherman bearing down on him. Agent Nurdler wasn't waiting. With a terrible scream he headed for the wire and went up it with an agility that was unnatural to him. He was over the top and running like mad through the trees when the tank veered away from the fence and returned to its original position. The lights went out and apart from Uncle Wally demanding at a thousand decibels to know when in thirty years of marriage he'd ever tried to sodomise Auntie Joan peace reigned. The Immelmann Intruder Deterrent had worked perfectly.

The audiovisual equipment in the Starfighter Mansion was working perfectly too. Every detail of the activities in the house was being monitored in the Surveillance Truck in the drive-in and while the bathroom sequence starring Auntie Joan on the can was all too revealing, the other people seemed to be behaving according to schedule, the schedule already firmly established in the minds of the DEA agents. Wally Immelmann was in his den chewing a cigar and alternately pacing up and down the room and helping himself to Scotch. Every now and then he picked up the phone to call his lawyer and then thought better of it and put it down again. He was obviously extremely worried about something.

'You think he smells us?' Murphy asked Palowski. 'Some guys got sixth sense. They can feel they're under surveillance. Remember that Panamanian down in Florida who was into voodoo. He was uncanny.'

'Man marries a broad like Mrs Immelmann doesn't have sixth sense. No way. Got no sense at all.'

'They say behind every rich man there's a great woman,' said Murphy.

'Great? Great doesn't get near it. This time it's gigantic.'

They switched to the quads who were busy filling their exercise books with details of Auntie Joan and Uncle Wally's sexual habits for their project on American culture for their English teacher.

'How do you spell "sodomise"?' asked Emmeline.

'Sodom and eye ess ee,' Samantha told her.

'Uncle Wally's really sexist. Talking about her thing like that is horrible.'

'Uncle Wally is a wally and he is horrible. They're both out-of-this-world awful. All that stuff he told us about the War and burning the Japanese with that flame thing. What did he call it?'

'A turkey roast on the hoof,' said Josephine.

'It sounds absolutely horrible. I'm never going to touch turkey again. I'll always associate them with little Japanese.'

'Not all Japanese are little,' Penelope pointed out. 'Some of those wrestlers are fearfully fat.'

'Like Auntie Joan,' said Samantha. 'She's disgusting.'

In the surveillance truck across the road Palowski and Murphy nodded agreement.

The next remark was of a different and more intriguing sort.

'I don't know why we're writing all this down now. The incriminating evidence is all there on the tape.'

'Miss Sprockett would have a fit if we played that to

the class. She's as butch as can be. I'd like to hear her opinion of Uncle Wally.'

'It's just a pity we haven't got it on video,' said Emmeline. 'Uncle Wally trying to find Auntie Joan's "thing" and giving it to her up the bum. We could make our fortunes.'

'We could have made our fortunes if you'd done what I wanted instead of putting the backup tape on the sound system,' Josephine said. 'I wonder what it sounds like. It's long past six. Uncle Wally's going to go absolutely bananas. He'd have paid a terrific amount of money for that tape. An absolute fortune. I mean if people find out—'

'If?' said Emmeline. 'I'd say he'll kill us when he finds out.'

But Samantha shook her head. 'He won't,' she said smugly. 'I've hidden the original tape where he'll never find it.'

'Where?' the others demanded but Samantha wasn't telling.

'Just somewhere he's never going to find it. I'm not telling you anything else. Emmy might go and tell him.'

'I wouldn't. You know I wouldn't,' said the aggrieved Emmeline.

'You said that when we put that stuff on the Revd Vascoe's computer and then you—'

'It wasn't me. It was Penny said I was the one who put it there.'

'Well, so you did. You were the one thought of it. And

anyway I didn't tell Mummy. She knows you because you're always the one who fouls things up.'

'I don't care about that,' said Samantha. 'And I'm still not telling and no one is going to make me. So there.'

The discussion moved on to the coming visit to the Florida Keys. Uncle Wally had said he wanted to take them shark fishing in his boat and Auntie Joan and Eva wanted to fly to Miami to do some shopping.

But downstairs Wally Immelmann's plans were being altered by the second.

'You telling me someone's tried to burglarise the Bear Fort?' he shouted down the phone at Sheriff Stallard who had got back to Wilma and had partially recovered his hearing and had called to find out how to get in touch with Mr Immelmann.

'I don't know about burglarising,' the Sheriff shouted back. 'All I know is there's a guy over Lossville says he's going to sue for nuisance and contravention of the Obscenity Regulations. Had difficulty hearing him myself.'

'Must be the fucking bears have set the system off. That guy is always complaining. And what's he mean about Obscenity Regulations? It's only a prolonged Frankie Sinatra. He sings "My Way".'

'If you say so, Mr Immelmann, I guess I got to believe you,' said the Sheriff. 'Though frankly—'

'I lie. The tape I got on is Abba. The Abba group. Real soothing stuff from way back.'

For a moment Sheriff Stallard hesitated. He didn't

want to cross Wally Immelmann but if that was Abba and real soothing his name wasn't Harry Stallard.

'Anyway, I'm just calling to ask you to cut the stuff off. You got a remote control or something?'

'A remote control? Are you crazy? There's no remote control can cover twenty-five miles with forest and mountains in between. You think I can bounce it off a satellite.'

'I guess I thought you might have some way of shutting it off,' said the Sheriff.

'Not from here I haven't. Got myself a generator so the power can't be cut off. Anyhow, what's it to you?'

Sheriff Stallard decided the time had come to break the news. 'I mean, what you and Mrs Immelmann are discussing over that sound system you've built up there isn't something you'd want to hear. The guy in Lossville says—'

'Fuck the little shit,' said Wally. 'I told you he is always complaining.' He paused. The Sheriff's last statement had hit him. 'What do you mean, what me and Mrs Immelmann are discussing?'

Sheriff Stallard gritted his teeth. This was going to be the hard bit. 'I don't really like to say, sir,' he muttered. 'It's kind of intimate.'

'Intimate?' Wally yelled. 'Are you fucking drunk or mad or something? Me and Mrs Immelmann?'

The Sheriff had had enough. He was getting real mad now. 'And Dr Cohen!' he shouted back. There was a gasp and silence on the line. 'You still there, Mr Immelmann?'

155

Mr Immelmann was still there. Just. He just wasn't hearing right. He couldn't be.

'What was that last you said?' he asked finally and in a weak voice.

'I said you and Mrs Immelmann are discussing intimate personal details about . . . well, I guess you know what you were talking about.'

'Like what?' Wally demanded.

'Well, like Dr Cohen and—'

'Shit!' yelled Wally. 'You telling me the bastard over in Lossville . . . oh, my God!'

'He called in to say it was all over the district up there, and we thought you might want to know.'

'I might want to know? I might want . . . What else did he say?'

'Could you cut it off is what he really wanted because the noise is driving his wife crazy. And what you and Mrs Immelmann are shouting about, like your sex life and what she didn't want you to do to her, isn't helping.'

Wally could well imagine it. The knowledge was driving him crazy too, trying to work out how what he and Joanie had said in the bedroom was coming out of the sound system at a thousand decibels plus. It wasn't possible.

'The thing is, there has to be some way to shut it down,' the Sheriff insisted. 'We got the National Guard team moving in. Maybe . . . Mr Immelmann, are you all right?'

Something in the Starfighter Mansion had crashed on to something else, like a table.

'Mr Immelmann, Mr Immelmann, oh shit!' shouted the Sheriff. 'Baxter, get an ambulance over there fast. Sounds like Wally's had a heart attack.'

20

There are in parts of most English industrial towns areas of such urban dereliction that only the most desperately self-pitying junkies and alcoholics, the discards of a concerned and caring society, choose to live there. A few old people, who would rather live anywhere else but can't afford to move, inhabit the top floors of the tower blocks and curse the day the local authority demolished their nineteenth-century back-to-backs in the 1960s ostensibly in the interests of health and hygiene. More correctly, in the interests of ambitious architects anxious to earn reputations and of local councillors anxious to line their pockets with hand-outs from developers whose only interest was in making vast profits.

One of these areas is on the edge of Ipford and it was towards this that Mrs Rottecombe drove. She knew the place fairly well, too well for her ever to mention it now. One of her first long list of clients before she had married Harold Rottecombe had had a cottage ten miles from Ipford and she had spent weekends there. When the customer had most inconsiderately gone to his Maker while on the job she had moved hurriedly to London to avoid the inquest. She had changed her name and had adopted that of a maternal aunt who had Alzheimer's and was incapable of remembering who she herself was let alone whether her niece was her daughter or not. The ruse worked. After that, it was simply a question of finding a respectable husband, and being a shrewd and ambitious woman she had made the acquaintance of Harold Rottecombe by becoming a worker in his local constituency office. From there to the Registry Office had been an easy task. Harold, for all his political acumen, had no idea what he had married. He would never know unless . . . unless it came to a divorce. In short, Ruth Rottecombe, reverting to the language of her adolescence, 'had him by the balls'. And the further he climbed the greasy pole of politics the less he would want her past to become public knowledge. So far, the only mistake she had made was in associating with Bob Battleby. And, of course, in having to get rid of the man in the back of the Volvo in such a way that he couldn't talk or, if he did, no one would believe him. Whoever he was, her instincts told her he was an educated married man and not a reporter for some filthy tabloid. Trying to explain to his wife or the police how he had lost his trousers was not going to be an easy one.

By the time she reached Ipford it was getting dark. She skirted the town and approached the derelict estate by a back road. The place was far worse than she'd remembered. There was no one about and no lights in any of the windows, most of which were boarded up. Illiterates with spray cans had covered walls with obscene graffiti. Ruth pulled into a dark alleyway where there were no street lights, parked under a looming tower block and switched off the Volvo estate. She got out and looked cautiously around her and up at the black or boarded-up windows on either side of the alley. In the distance she could hear the sound of lorries on the motorway but otherwise there was no sound of life. Three minutes later she had removed the newspapers and cardboard boxes, unwrapped the Elastoplast from his wrists and removed the gag, and was dragging Wilt by the feet into the gutter, in the process banging his head on the kerb. Then she slammed the back of the estate and drove on only to find she was in a cul-de-sac. She reversed the car and drove back the way she had come, her headlights picking out the almost naked figure of Wilt. She was glad to see his head had begun to bleed again. What she didn't see was a plywood board covering a window standing partly open on the second floor of the tower block above as she turned right and headed for the motorway. She was by this time tired but euphoric. She had rid herself of a dangerous threat to Harold's reputation and her own influence. What she forgot as she drove back to Meldrum Slocum was to get rid of Wilt's jeans, boots, socks and rucksack which were still under the cardboard boxes. By the time she reached Leyline Lodge she was exhausted and slumped into bed. Far behind her the plywood board in the tower block had long since closed again.

An hour later a group of drunk skinheads passed the head of the alley, spotted the body and came up to have a look at it.

'A bloody old poofter,' said one of them, drawing the conclusion from the lack of Wilt's jeans. 'Let's put the boot in.' And having expressed their feelings for gays by kicking him in the ribs a few times and once in the face, they staggered off laughing. Wilt felt nothing. He had found an Older England than he'd expected but he still didn't know it.

A feeble dawn had broken when he was found by a police car. Two constables got out and looked down at him.

'Best call an ambulance. This one's a right mess. Tell them it's urgent.'

While the WPC used the car radio the other looked around. Above his head the plywood board opened.

'Happened around three hours ago,' said an old woman. 'A woman in a white car came and dragged him out. Then some young bastards gave him a kicking just for the fun of it.'

The constable peered up at her. 'You should have called us, mother,' he said.

'What with, I'd like to know? Think I've got a phone?'

'Don't suppose you have. What are you doing here anyway? Last time you were down the road.'

The old woman poked her head further out. 'Think I'm staying in one place round here? Not likely. I may be cabbage-looking but I ain't that green. Got to keep moving so those young swine don't get me.'

The policeman took out a notebook. 'Get a look at the number-plate of the car?' he asked.

'What, in this dark? Course I didn't. Saw a woman though. Rich bitch by the look of her. Not from round here.'

'We can drive you down with us to the station. You'll be safe enough down there.'

'I don't mean that. I want to go back where I came from. That's what I mean, copper.'

But before the constable could ask where that was the Woman Police Officer returned with the news that no ambulances were available. There had been a major accident involving two coaches full of schoolchildren on a trip abroad, a petrol tanker and a lorry carrying pigs on the motorway twenty miles away and every available ambulance and fire engine had been sent to the scene.

'Pigs?' queried the constable.

'At least they think it was pigs. The Duty Sergeant's been told the smell of roast pork is appalling.'

'Never mind about that. What about the school kids?'

'They're in the ambulances. The two coaches skidded on the pig fat and turned over,' the WPC told him.

'Oh well, we'd better put this bastard in the back of the car and take him down the hospital ourselves.'

Above their heads the old woman had closed the plywood board again and disappeared. With Wilt lying prone on the back seat they drove to Ipford General Hospital and met with a hostile reception.

'Oh, all right,' said a distraught doctor called by the nurse in A & E. 'It will be difficult with this damned accident. We haven't any spare beds. We haven't even a spare trolley. I'm not even sure we've got any spare corridors, and just to make working in what amounts to a human abattoir so fulfilling, we've got a major catastrophe on our hands, four doctors off sick and the usual shortage of nursing staff. Why can't you take him home? He's less likely to die there.'

All the same, Wilt was finally lifted on to a stretcher, and space in a long corridor was found for him. Fortunately, Wilt was still unconscious.

21

Uncle Wally was not so lucky. He was fully conscious and wishing to hell he wasn't. He had come out of Intensive Care, had refused to see Auntie Joanie and was having a most unpleasant conversation with Dr Cohen who was telling him a man of his age . . . well, a man of any age deserved an infarct if he did what he'd done to his wife or any other person for that matter. It was, he said, *contra natura*.

'Contra what?' Wally gasped. The only Contras he'd heard of had fought the Sandinistas in Nicaragua.

'Against nature. The sphincter is designed to let excreta out not—'

'Shit! What's excrecha?'

'What you just said. Shit,' said Dr Cohen. 'Now, like I was saying, the sphincter—'

'I don't even know what a sphincter is.'

'Asshole,' said Dr Cohen ambiguously.

Wally took umbrage. 'You calling me an asshole?' he yelled.

Dr Cohen hesitated. Wally Immelmann might be a first-rate business man but . . . The guy was sick. He didn't want to kill the idiot.

'I am merely trying to explain the physiological

consequences of putting . . . putting things up someone's anus instead of in the normal way.'

Wally gaped at him and turned a nasty colour. He couldn't find words for his feelings.

Dr Cohen continued. 'Not only could you give your dear wife Aids but—'

Wally Immelmann found words. 'Aids?' he yelled. 'What's all this about my having Aids? I haven't got Aids. I'm not a faggot.'

'I'm not saying you are. I don't care. What you do is your own business. I am merely telling you that what you have been doing to your wife can be physically damaging to her. Not can be. Is. She could be wearing tampons the rest of her life.'

'Who says I do what you're saying I do to her?' demanded Wally inadvisedly.

Dr Cohen sighed. He'd had just about all he could stomach from Wally Immelmann. 'As a matter of fact you do,' he snapped. 'You can be heard miles away shouting at Mrs Immelmann about giving it to her up the ass. People are taking tours up near Lake Sassaquassee just to hear you.'

Wally's eyes bulged in his suffused face. 'You mean . . . oh my God, they haven't cut the loudspeakers off? They've got to.'

'You tell them how. The police can't get near the place. They've had the National Guard and helicopters and . . .'

But Wally Immelmann was no longer listening. He'd

had another infarct. As he was rushed back to Intensive Care, Dr Cohen left the hospital. He was a kindly man and gays could do what they liked but screwing wives anally when they didn't like it disgusted him.

At the Starfighter Mansion things weren't much better. Auntie Joan had taken to her bed and had locked the door, only unlocking it to go down to the kitchen to get her breakfast, lunch and dinner. She and Eva were hardly on speaking terms and the quads had taken over Uncle Wally's computer and were sending email messages to all their friends and a number of obscene ones to all recipients on his business address list. Eva, who knew nothing about computers and was in any case too worried about her Henry, left them to their own and Uncle Wally's devices. She spent her time on the phone to England calling up friends, even Mavis Mottram, to find out where he'd got to. Nobody knew.

'But he can't just have disappeared. That's not possible.'

'No, dear, and I didn't say he'd disappeared,' said Mavis with mock sympathy. 'I just said nobody knew where he was.'

'But that's the same as saying he's disappeared,' said Eva, who had learnt some elements of logic from Wilt during their frequent arguments. 'You said nobody knows where he is. Someone has to know. I mean, he may have gone on holiday with the Braintrees. Have you tried them?'

At the other end of the line Mavis took a deep breath.

She had always found Eva difficult to deal with and she wasn't prepared to be grilled by her now.

'No,' she said. 'I haven't. For the simple reason that I don't know their address or if they have gone on holiday and I'm hardly likely to know where they've gone.'

'They always take a cottage in Norfolk for a month in the summer.'

This time Mavis didn't breathe deeply. She snorted. 'Then why don't you phone them?' she snapped.

'Because I don't know where the cottage is. All I do know is that it's in Norfolk somewhere on the coast.'

'Norfolk?' squawked Mavis. 'If you seriously think I'm going to start searching cottages along the entire coast of Norfolk . . . well, it's out of the question. Why don't you phone the hospitals and the police? They've usually kept an eye on your Henry. Ask for Missing Persons.'

All in all it was a most disagreeable and acrimonious exchange, and it ended with Mavis putting the phone down without saying goodbye. Eva tried the house again but all she got was her own voice on the answerphone. Apart from the quads, and she wasn't going to worry them, Eva had no one to consult. Upstairs Auntie Joan could be heard snoring. She'd taken another sleeping pill and washed it down with Jack Daniels. Eva went out to the kitchen. At least there she could talk to Maybelle, the black maid, and tell her her problems. Even that didn't help. Maybelle's experience with men was even worse than Eva's.

'Men's all the same. The second you turn your back

they's off like alley cats chasing other girls.'

'But my Henry's not like that. He's . . . well, he's different from other men. And he's definitely not gay, if that's what you're thinking.' Maybelle had raised her eyebrows significantly. 'It's just that he's not really interested in sex,' Eva confided.

'Then he's gotta be different. Never met a man like that in all my life. That Mr Immelmann sure isn't. I reckon that's how come his heart's so bad.' She looked out the window. 'There's those men again. I don't know what they think they're doing snooping round the house all the time. And Mrs Joanie's lost her voice or something. Comes down and gets herself some ice cream and brownies and goes on back up to her room and never a word out of her. Guess she's all upset over Mr Immelmann being took bad.'

Up at the lake a blessed silence reigned. A special squad of totally deaf Gulf War veterans had been recruited to destroy the generator with explosives. Even then they had found the task difficult and had had to use clothing that looked like spacesuits to get near the thing. But in the end they had succeeded. The loudspeakers went dead and the Drug Squad moved in and ransacked the place. They found nothing more incriminating than a stack of porno videos hidden in Wally's safe. But by the time they left, the house looked as though it had been vandalised.

22

But it was in the Starfighter Mansion in Wilma that the real battle was about to begin. Auntie Joanie had woken from her pill-induced sleep determined to visit Wally and had driven down to the hospital only to learn that he was in Intensive Care and could see no one. Dr Cohen and the chief cardiologist broke the news to her.

'He's not unconscious but his condition is exceedingly grave. We're thinking of having him transferred to the South Atlanta Heart Clinic,' the cardiologist told her.

'But that's where they do heart transplants!' Joanie shrieked. 'He can't be that bad.'

'It's just that we haven't the facilities here in Wilma. He'll be a heap better off at the Clinic.'

'Well, I'm going there with him. I'm not having him have a heart transplant without my being with him.'

'No one is talking about a heart transplant, Mrs Immelmann. It's just that he'll get the best treatment possible down there.'

'I don't care!' she screamed inconsequentially. 'I'm going to be with him to the end. You can't stop me.'

'Nobody's going to stop you. You're entitled to go where you like, but I won't take responsibility for the consequences,' said the cardiologist and ended the argument by going back to Intensive Care.

As she drove back to the Starfighter Mansion in a blazing temper she made up her mind what she was going to do. Tell Eva to get herself and her brats out of the house.

'I'm going down to Atlanta with Wally!' she shouted. 'And you're going back to England and I never want to see you, any of you, ever again. Pack up and go.'

For once Eva agreed with her. The visit had been a disaster and besides, she was frantically worried about Henry. She should never have left him alone. He was bound to have got into trouble without her. She told the quads to pack their things and get ready to leave. But they had heard Auntie Joan shouting and were way ahead of her. The only problem was how to get to the airport. Eva put the question to Auntie Joan when she stormed downstairs.

'Get a bloody cab, you bitch,' she snapped.

'But I haven't the money,' said Eva pathetically.

'Oh, God. Never mind. Anything to get you out of the house.' She went to the phone and called the cab company and presently the Wilts were on their way. The quads said nothing. They knew better than to talk when Eva was in this sort of mood.

In the Surveillance Truck Murphy and Palowski were uncertain what to do. No trace of any drug had been detected in the effluent coming from the Starfighter Mansion. Wally Immelmann's heart attack had made the situation even more difficult and what they had seen and heard in the house didn't suggest any activity connected with drugs. Domestic murder seemed more likely.

'Best call Atlanta and tell them the sumo with quadruplets is coming and let them decide the action,' said Murphy.

'Affirmative,' Palowski agreed. He'd forgotten how to say yes.

23

In Ipford General Hospital Wilt still hadn't come round. He'd been moved from the corridor to make room for six youngsters injured in the pig inferno. Finally after forty-eight hours Wilt was taken into X-ray and diagnosed as suffering from severe concussion and three badly bruised ribs, but there was no sign of a fractured skull. From there he was wheeled to what was called the Neurological Ward. As usual it was full.

'Of course it was a crime,' said the Duty Sergeant grumpily when the doctor at the hospital phoned the police station to ask what exactly had happened. 'The bugger was mugged and dumped unconscious in the street behind the New Estate. What he was doing there we've no idea. Probably drunk or . . . well, your guess is as good as mine. He wasn't wearing any trousers. Being in that district he was asking for it.'

'Any identity?' the doctor asked.

'One of our men saw him and thought he recognised him as a lecturer at the Tech. Name of Wilt. Mr Henry Wilt. He taught Communications Studies and—'

'So what's his address? Oh, never mind, you can

inform his relatives he's been mugged and is in Ipford Hospital.' And he rang off angrily.

In his office Inspector Flint leapt to his feet and barged into the passage. 'Did I hear you say "Henry Wilt"?'

The Sergeant nodded. 'He's up at the hospital. Been mugged according to some quack who . . .'

But Flint was no longer listening. He hurried down to the police station car park and headed for the hospital.

It was a frustrated Inspector Flint who finally found Wilt in the overcrowded maze that was Ipford General Hospital. To begin with he'd been directed to Neurology only to find Wilt had been moved to Vasectomy.

'What on earth for? I understood he had been mugged. What's he need a vasectomy for?'

'He doesn't. He was only here temporarily. Then he was taken to Hysterectomy.'

'Hysterectomy? Dear God,' said Flint faintly. He could just begin to understand why a man who must presumably have been an active participant in helping to foist those dreadful quads on the world might deserve a vasectomy to prevent him inflicting any more nightmares; hysterectomy was something else again. 'But the blighter's a man. You can't give a man a hysterectomy. It's not possible.'

'That's why he was moved to Infectious Diseases 3. They had a spare bed there. At least I think it was ID 3,' the nurse told him. 'I know someone died there this morning. Mind you, they always do.'

'Why?' asked Flint incautiously.

'Aids,' said the nurse, pushing an obese woman on a trolley past him.

'But they can't put a man who's been beaten up and is bleeding in the same bed as a bloke who's just died of Aids. It's outrageous. Bloody near condemning him to death.'

'Oh, they sterilise the sheets and all that,' said the nurse over her shoulder.

It was a pale, frustrated and appalled Inspector who finally found Wilt in Unisex 8 which was reserved for geriatrics who had had a variety of operations that required them to wear catheters, drips and in several cases tubes protruding from various other orifices. Flint couldn't see why it was called a unisex ward. Multi-sex would have been more accurate though just as unpleasant. To take his attention away from a patient of indeterminate sex – for once Flint preferred the politically correct word 'gender' – who clearly had an almost continuous incontinence problem and what amounted to a phobic horror of catheters, the Inspector tried to concentrate on Wilt. His condition was pretty awful too. His scalp was bandaged and his face badly bruised and swollen but the Ward Sister assured Flint that he'd soon recover consciousness. Flint said he sincerely hoped so.

Shortly afterwards the old man in the next bed had convulsions and his false teeth fell out. A nurse put them back and called the Sister who took her time coming.

'What's the matter with you?' she demanded. Even to Flint's medically untutored way of thinking, the question seemed gratuitous. How the hell could the old fellow know what was wrong with him?

'How would I know? I just get these hot flushes. I had a prostate operation on Tuesday,' he said.

'And a very successful one too. You've done nothing but grumble since you came here. You're just a grotty old man. I'll be glad to see the back of you.'

The nurse intervened. 'But he's eighty-one, Sister,' she said.

'And a very healthy eighty-one he is too,' the Sister replied and swept off to deal with the patient who had dragged his catheter out for the fifth time. It was perfectly obvious what 'gender' he was now. To avoid witnessing the reinsertion of the catheter, and a fresh bout of convulsions by the old man in the next bed, Flint turned to look at Wilt and found an eye staring at him. Wilt had recovered consciousness and, if the eye was anything to go by, didn't like what he was seeing. Flint wasn't enjoying it much either. He stared back and wondered what to do. But the eye closed abruptly. Flint turned to the nurse to ask her if an open eye was an indication that the patient had recovered consciousness but the nurse was having difficulty putting the old man's dentures back into his mouth again. When she had succeeded Flint asked again.

'Couldn't say, not really,' she said. 'I've known some of them die with their eyes wide open. Of course they glaze over a bit blue later on. That way you know they've gone.'

'Charming,' said the Inspector and turned back but Wilt's eyes were firmly shut. The sight of the Inspector sitting beside the bed had so startled him he had almost forgotten his dreadful headache and how awful he felt. Whatever had happened to him – and he had no idea where he'd been or what he'd done – the vaguely familiar figure sitting and staring at him was not a reassuring one. Not that he recognised Flint. And presently he fell into a coma again and Flint sent for Sergeant Yates.

'I'm off home for a bit of lunch and a kip,' he told him. 'Let me know the moment he comes round and on no account let that idiot Hodge know he's here. He'll have Wilt charged for drug dealing before the poor bugger's conscious.'

He went down the seemingly endless corridors and drove home.

24

On the other side of the Atlantic Eva and the quads sat in the airport waiting for their plane. It had been delayed first by a bomb threat and then, when it had been thoroughly searched, by a mechanical fault. Eva was no longer impatient or even angry with the quads or Auntie Joan. She was glad to be going home to her Henry but intensely worried about his whereabouts and what had happened to him. The girls played and squabbled around her. She blamed herself for having accepted the invitation to Wilma but at least she was going home and in a way she was glad her mission to get the Immelmanns to change their wills in the girls' favour had failed so catastrophically. The prospect of a fortune would have been bad for the quads.

From an office overlooking the check-in DEA officials studied the little group and wondered what to do.

'We stop them here, we're not going to find anything. If there ever was anything to find. Reckon Palowski was right. This Mrs Wilt is a decoy. The guys in London can check her out. No point in pulling her in here.'

What Ruth Rottecombe was doing was preparing a prospect that would be very bad. For Wilt, at any rate.

When she was woken from her sleep after her long drive back from Ipford by a phone call from the Superintendent at Oston Police Station to say he was coming up to interview her, she realised she hadn't got rid of Wilt's trousers and rucksack as she had intended. They were still in the back of the Volvo. If the police found them . . . Ruth preferred not to think of the consequences. She hurried out to the garage and took them up to an empty trunk in the attic and locked it. Then she returned to the garage and moved the car over the spot where Wilt had fallen and locked Wilfred and Pickles inside. They would act as a deterrent to any investigation of the place. Somehow she had been sure the police would pay her another visit and she had no wish to answer any more awkward questions.

She need not have worried. The police had checked at the Country Club and Battleby's alibi seemed authentic. He had been there at least an hour before the fire had broken out and the arson investigators had found no sign of a delayed-action device. Whoever had started the fire, it couldn't have been the beastly Battleby or Mrs Rottecombe. And they'd got the bloody paedophile on two charges, one of which would put him away for a very long time and ruin the swine's reputation for life. The Superintendent didn't care so much about the arson. On the other hand, while he detested Ruthless Ruth, he had to be careful. She was the wife of an influential Member of Parliament who could ask awkward questions in the House about police interrogation methods and harassment. It would pay to be polite to her for the time being. Talking about the fire would give him a chance to study her.

'I'm extremely sorry to bother you,' he said when she opened the front door. 'It's just that there are some points in the case against Mr Battleby that are bothering us and we thought you might be in a position to enlighten us. We are simply concerned with the fire at the Manor House.'

Ruth Rottecombe hesitated for a moment and decided to be conciliatory. 'If I can be of any help, I'll certainly try. You'd better come in.'

She held the door open but the Superintendent was not anxious to enter a house if those damned bull terriers were loose inside. It had taken all his courage to drive up and get out of the car.

'About those two dogs . . .' he began but Mrs Rottecombe reassured him.

'They are locked in the garage. Do come in.'

They went into the drawing room.

'Please take a seat.'

The Superintendent sat down hesitantly. This was hardly the reception he'd expected. Mrs Rottecombe pulled up a chair and prepared to answer questions.

The Superintendent picked his words carefully. 'We have checked with the Club Secretary and he has confirmed that Battleby was at the Country Club playing bridge for nearly an hour before the fire broke out. Secondly, the kitchen door was unlocked. So it was perfectly possible that someone else started the fire.'

'But that's impossible. I locked—' Ruth said before realising she was walking into a trap. 'I mean, someone must have known where the keys were kept. I hope you don't think I—'

'Certainly not,' said the Superintendent. 'We know you were at the Club at the same time. No, there's no suspicion against you. I can guarantee that. What interests us more is a set of footprints in the vegetable garden. They are those of a man who came down from the track behind the house. Now in the mud in the track we've also found tyre marks which indicate that a vehicle was parked there and drove off hurriedly some time later on. It begins to look as though the fire was started deliberately by a third party.'

Mrs Rottecombe bridled at that 'third'. 'Are you suggesting Bob hired someone to start the fire—'

'I'm not suggesting anything,' said the Superintendent hurriedly. 'I simply meant that someone, some unknown person, entered the house and caused the fire. We also have evidence that he had been in the kitchen garden for some considerable time, evidently watching the house. There are a group of footprints by the gate in the wall which indicate that he had moved about waiting for a chance to enter the house.' He paused. 'What we are trying to find out is if anyone had a particular grudge against the man Battleby, and we wondered if you could help us.'

Mrs Rottecombe nodded. 'I should think there were a great many,' she said finally. 'Bob Battleby was not a popular figure in the district. Those vile magazines in the Range Rover indicate that he has paedophile tendencies and he may have abused . . . well, done something horrible.'

It was her turn to pause and let the inference sink in. The suggestion helped to clear her of any connection with that side of Battleby's inclinations. Whatever she was she was not a child or, as the Superintendent put it to himself, a spring chicken.

By the time he left he had not gained any useful information from her. On the other hand, Ruth Rottecombe had a shrewd idea why Harold had found the unconscious man in the garage. He'd had something to do with that disastrous night and she saw no reason why she shouldn't provide the police with his jeans covered with ash near the burnt-out Manor. She wouldn't leave them there immediately but would wait until it was dark. Like after midnight.

25

When Wilt opened his eyes again Flint was still in the chair beside the bed. The Inspector had shut his own eyes when the old man in the next bed spat his dentures out for the fifth time and accompanied them with such a quantity of blood that some of it had landed on his trousers. After that he had ceased to be a grotty old man of eighty-one and was a decidedly dead one. Wilt had heard Flint say 'Fuck' and various unpleasant noises going on but had kept his eyes firmly shut, only opening them in time to see Flint turn and look at him curiously.

'Feeling better, Henry?' Flint asked.

Wilt didn't reply. The police waiting to take a statement from him weren't at all to his liking. And in any case Wilt had no idea what had happened to him or what he might have done. It seemed best to have amnesia. Besides, he wasn't feeling any better. If anything Flint's presence made him feel decidedly worse. But before the Inspector could make any more inquiries a doctor came up to the bed. This time it was Flint who was questioned.

'What are you doing here?' the doctor asked rather nastily, evidently disliking the presence of a police officer in the ward almost as much as Wilt did. Flint wasn't enjoying being there either.

'Waiting to take a statement from this patient,' he said, indicating Wilt.

'Well, you're not likely to get one out of him today. He's suffering from severe concussion and probably amnesia. He may not remember anything. That's a frequent consequence of a severe blow to the head and subsequent concussion.'

'And how long does one have to wait before he gets his memory back?'

'Depends. I've known some cases where there's been no return at all. That's rare, of course, but it does occasionally happen. Frankly, there's no saying but in this case I should think he'll get some memories back in a day or two.'

Wilt listened to the exchange and made it a day or three. He had to find out what he had done first.

Eva returned to 45 Oakhurst Avenue in a state of total exhaustion. The flight had been awful, a drunk had had to be tied down for hitting another passenger and the plane had been diverted to Manchester because of a breakdown in the Flight Control computer. What she found when she finally got home temporarily galvanised her. The house looked as though it had been burgled. Wilt's ordinary clothes, along with his shoes, were scattered on the floor of the bedroom and to add to her alarm several drawers in the bedroom had obviously been clumsily searched. The same was true of the desk in his study. Finally, and in its own way most alarming of all, the mail had been opened and lay on a side-table beside the front door. While the quads, still relatively subdued, went upstairs she phoned the Tech only to be told by the Secretary that he hadn't been seen there and there was no saying where he was. Eva put the phone down and tried the Braintrees' number. They were bound to know where he was. There was no answer. She pressed the button on the answerphone and heard herself repeatedly telling Henry to phone her in Wilma. She went back upstairs and felt in the pockets of Wilt's clothes but there was nothing to indicate what he had been doing or where he was. The fact that they were lying in a pile on the floor frightened her. She'd trained him to fold them up carefully and he'd got into the habit of hanging them over the back of a chair. From there she went to the wardrobe and checked his other trousers and jackets. None of them were missing. He must have been wearing something when he left the house. He couldn't have gone out naked. Eva's thoughts ran wildly to extremes. Ignoring Penelope's questions she went back downstairs and phoned the police station.

'I want to report a missing person,' she said. 'My name is Mrs Wilt and I've just got back from America and my husband is missing.'

'When you say missing do you mean—'

'I'm saying he has disappeared.'

'In America?' asked the girl.

'Not in America. I left him here and I live at 45 Oakhurst Avenue. I've just come back and he isn't here.'

'If you'll just hold the line a moment.' The telephonist could be heard muttering to someone in the background about some ghastly woman and she could understand why her husband had gone missing. 'I'll put you through to someone who may be able to help you,' she said.

'You lousy bitch, I heard what you just said!' yelled Eva.

'Me? I didn't say anything. And I'll have you for using offensive language.'

In the end she was answered by Sergeant Yates. 'Is that Mrs Eva Wilt of 45 Oakhurst Avenue?'

'Who else do you think it is?' Eva snapped back.

'I'm afraid I have some rather bad news for you, Mrs Wilt. Your husband has been in some sort of accident,' the Sergeant told her. He obviously didn't like being snapped at. 'He's in the Ipford General Hospital and he's still unconscious. If you . . .'

But Eva had already slammed the phone down and, having told the quads in her most menacing manner to behave themselves really well, was on her way to the hospital. She parked and stormed through the crowded waiting room to the reception desk, pushing aside a little man who was already there.

'You'll just have to wait your turn,' the girl told her.

'But my husband has been injured in a serious accident and he's unconscious. I've got to see him.'

'You'd better try A & E then.'

'A & E? What's that?' Eva demanded.

'Accident and Emergency. It's out the main door. You'll see a sign,' said the receptionist and attended to the little man.

Eva hurried out the door and turned left. There was no sign of Accident and Emergency there. Cursing the receptionist she tried to the right. It wasn't there either. In the end she asked a woman with her arm in a sling and was directed to the other end of the hospital.

'It's way past the main door. You can't miss it. I wouldn't go in, though. It's absolutely filthy. Dust everywhere.'

This time Eva did find it. The place was filled with children injured in the coach crash. Eva went back to the main door and found herself in what looked like a shopping mall with a restaurant and adjacent tearoom, a boutique, a parfumerie and a book and magazine stall. For a moment she felt quite mad. Then gathering her wits together she headed down a passage following a sign which read 'Gynaecology'. There were more signs pointing down other corridors further on. Henry wouldn't be in a gynaecological ward.

Eva stopped a man in a white coat who was carrying a decidedly sinister-looking plastic bucket with a blood-stained cloth over it.

'Can't stop now. I've got to get this little tot to the incinerator. We've got another starting in twenty minutes.'

'Another baby? That's lovely,' said Eva without getting the implication of 'the incinerator'.

The nurse put her right. 'Another bloody foetus,' he said. 'Take a dekko if you don't believe me.'

He removed the bloodstained cloth and Eva glanced into the bucket. As the nurse hurried away she fainted and slid down the wall. Opposite her a door opened and a young doctor, a very young doctor, came out. The fact that he was a Lithuanian and had recently attended a seminar on Obesity and Coronary Infarcts didn't help. Fat women lying unconscious were his chance to show his expertise. Five minutes later Eva Wilt was in the Emergency Heart Unit, had been stripped to her panties, was being given oxygen and was about to be put on a defibrillator. That didn't help either. She wasn't unconscious long. She woke to find a nurse lifting her breasts for a defibrillator pad. Eva promptly hit her and hurled herself off the trolley and grabbed her clothes and was out of the room. She dashed to the toilet and got dressed. She'd come to visit her Henry and nothing was going to stop her. After trying several other wards she traipsed back to Reception. This time she was told that Mr Wilt was in Psychiatry 3.

'Where's that?' Eva asked.

'On floor 6 at the far end,' the receptionist told her to get rid of the wretched woman. Eva looked for a lift, failed to find one and had to walk up to floor 6 only to find herself outside Autopsy. Even she knew what an autopsy was. But Henry wasn't dead. He was in Psychiatry 3. An hour later she found that he wasn't. In the following two hours she had walked another mile and was furious. So furious in fact that she tackled a senior surgeon and screamed abuse at him. Then because it was getting late she remembered the girls at home. She'd have to go back to see they weren't up to any mischief and to make supper. In any case she was too exhausted to continue her search for Henry. She'd try again in the morning.

26

But by the time she arrived at the hospital the next morning, Inspector Flint had gone to get a cup of coffee and Wilt was still apparently unconscious. In fact Wilt was considering what the doctor had said.

'He may have amnesia and have no memory of what happened to him.' Or words to that effect. Wilt was now definitely in favour of having amnesia. He'd had no intention of making a statement. He'd had an awful night, much of it spent listening to a man on a heart monitor by the door dying. At one o'clock the Night Sister had come to the ward and Wilt had heard her whisper to the Ward Nurse that they'd have to do something about the man because he was coupling and wouldn't last till morning if they didn't iron the problem out. Listening to the sounds of the monitor Wilt could hear what she meant. The beeps were most irregular and as the night wore on they got worse, until just before dawn they petered out altogether and he could hear the poor old fellow's bed being wheeled out into the corridor. For a moment he thought of looking over to see what was going on but there was no point. It would only be morbid curiosity to see the corpse being carted off to the morgue.

Instead he lay sadly pondering on the mystery of life

and death and wondering if there was anything in the 'near-death experience' and people who had seen the light at the end of the tunnel and a bearded old gentleman, God or someone, who led them into a beautiful garden before deciding they weren't to die after all. Either that or they hung around the ceiling of the operating theatre looking down at their own bodies and listening to what the surgeons had to say. Wilt couldn't see why they bothered. There must be something more interesting to do on the 'other side'. The notion that it was fascinating to eavesdrop on surgeons who'd just cocked up one's operation suggested the 'other side' didn't have much to offer in the way of interest. Not that Wilt had much confidence in the existence of the 'other side'. He'd read somewhere that surgeons had gone to the trouble of writing words on top of the theatre lampshade that could only be seen by people and flies on the ceiling to check if the 'near-death' patients could really have been up there. None of those who had come back had ever been able to quote what was written there. That was proof enough for Wilt. Besides, he'd read somewhere else that the 'near-death' experience could be induced by increasing carbon dioxide content in the brain. On the whole Wilt remained sceptical. Death might be a great adventure, as someone had once put it, but Wilt wasn't keen on it all the same. He was still wondering where the blighter by the door had got to, and whether he was chatting with some other newly dear departed or simply lying in the mortuary cooling gently and getting rigor mortis, when the Night Sister came round again. She was a tall and well-scrubbed woman who evidently liked her patients to be asleep.

'Why are you still awake?' she demanded.

Wilt looked at her bleakly and wondered if she always slept well. 'It's that poor bloke by the door,' he said finally.

'The poor bloke by the door? What on earth are you talking about? He's not making any noise.'

'I know that,' said Wilt, staring at her pathetically. 'I know he's not making any noise. Poor sod can't, can he? He's shuffled.'

'Shuffled?' said the Sister, looking at him curiously. 'What do you mean, he's shuffled?'

Wilt stared at her more pathetically still. 'Shuffled off this mortal coil,' he said.

'Shuffled off this mortal coil? What are you babbling about?'

Wilt took his time. Obviously the Sister didn't know her Shakespeare.

'Pegged it, for goodness' sake. Kicked the bucket. Dropped off the perch. Handed in his dinner pail. Crossed that bourn from which no traveller returns. Died.'

The Sister looked at him as though he really had gone mad. Gone mad or was delirious.

'Don't be so stupid. There's nothing the matter with him. It's the heart monitor that's gone wrong.'

And with a remark about 'some people' she passed on down the ward. Wilt peered in the direction of the door and was slightly aggrieved to see the man was still there sleeping peacefully. After what seemed ages he went to sleep himself. He was woken two hours later and presently a doctor examined him.

'What drugs were you on?' he asked.

Wilt stared at him blankly. 'I've never taken any drugs in my life,' he muttered.

The doctor looked at his notes. 'That's not what it says here. You were clearly on something during the night according to Sister Brownsel. Oh well, we'll soon find out with a blood test.'

Wilt said nothing. He was going back to suffering from amnesia and since he really couldn't remember what had happened to him he wouldn't be bluffing. All the same he was still worried. He had to find out what had been going on.

Eva arrived at the hospital accompanied by Mavis Mottram. Not that she liked Mavis but at least she was a dominant personality and would stand no nonsense from anyone. To begin with Mavis lived up to her hopes.

'Name,' she snapped at the girl at the reception desk and took out a small notebook. 'Name and address.'

'What do you want it for?'

'To report you to the Administrator for deliberately directing Mrs Wilt here to Psychiatry when you knew perfectly well where her husband was.'

The girl looked wildly around. Anything to get away from this gorgon.

Mavis went on. 'I happen to be a member of the council,' she said, omitting to mention that it was only the parish council, not the county council, 'and what's more I happen to know Dr Roche very well indeed.'

The receptionist went white. Dr Roche was the top physician and a very important man. She could see she was in danger of losing her job. 'Mr Wilt hadn't been logged in,' she muttered.

'And whose fault was that? Yours, of course,' said Mavis with a snarl and wrote something in her notebook. 'Now then, where is Mr Wilt?'

The receptionist checked the register and phoned someone. 'There's a woman here—'

'Lady, if you don't mind,' hissed Mavis.

Behind her Eva marvelled at Mavis Mottram's authority. 'I don't know how you do it,' she said. 'When I try it never works.'

'It's simply a question of breeding. My family can trace its lineage back to William the Conqueror.'

'Fancy that. And your father was a plumber too,' said Eva, unable to keep a note of scepticism out of her voice.

'And a very good one too. What was your father?'

'My daddy died when I was young,' said Eva mournfully.

'Quite. Barmen frequently do. Of drink.'

'He didn't. He died of pancreatitis.'

'And how do you get pancreatitis? By drinking whisky and gin by the gallon. In other words by becoming an alcoholic.'

Before the spat could turn into a full-scale row the receptionist intervened. 'Mr Wilt has been moved to Geriatrics 5,' she told them. 'You'll find it on the second floor. There's a lift just along the passage.'

'There had better be,' said Mavis and they set off. Five minutes later Mavis had another altercation, this time with a very formidable Sister who refused them entry on the grounds that it wasn't Visiting Hours. Even Mavis Mottram's insistence that Mrs Wilt was Mr Wilt's wife and entitled to see him at any time didn't have any effect. In the end they had to sit in the Waiting Room for two hours.

27

The discovery of Wilt's trousers covered with mud and what looked like dried blood, and with several holes burnt in them, in the lane behind the late Meldrum Manor interested the police at Oston.

'Ah, now we're getting somewhere. That bastard Battleby hired some swine to torch the place,' the Superintendent told the group of policemen assembled to find out what had really happened on the night of the fire. 'And what's more we've got the sod's name and address from an envelope in the back pocket. Name of Mr H. Wilt. Address 45 Oakhurst Avenue, Ipford. Does that ring a bell with any of you?'

A constable raised his hand. 'That's the name of the backpacker stayed at Mrs Rawley's B & B up Lentwood Way. You told me to check hotels. There aren't too many about these parts so I tried the bed and breakfasts too. He stayed at Mrs Crow's the night before. Wouldn't say where he was heading. Claimed he didn't know where he was and didn't want to know.'

A sergeant spoke up. 'My wife's from Ipford,' he said, 'and we get the *Weekly Echo*. There was a story in last week's about a man being found unconscious in the New Ipford Estate with his head bashed in and no trousers.

Covered in mud he was too.'

The Superintendent left the room and made a phone call.

'Thank you. Spot on,' he said when he returned. 'He's in the Ipford General with concussion and suffering from amnesia. They're waiting for him to come round. In the mean time they're sending a specimen of the mud on his shirt up for us to check if it's the same as in the lane back of the Manor.'

'That's strange. I went up that lane the very next day in broad daylight and there were no trousers there then. I guarantee that,' said a young constable. 'The insurance bods did the same. You can ask them.'

The Superintendent pursed his lips. What interested him was that the jeans had motor oil and blood on them. He still hadn't forgotten or forgiven Mrs Rottecombe's insulting attitude on the night of the fire. His 'nose' told him she was involved in the fire at Meldrum Manor in some way. And where had the Shadow Minister for Social Enhancement got to? The newspapers had taken their revenge with accusations that invited a suit for libel but there had not been a squeak out of the MP. Odd, very odd. But most suspicious of all the policeman ostensibly at the gate to guard Leyline Lodge but in fact to keep an eye on the house had reported that the garage doors hadn't been opened since Wilfred and Pickles had dealt with the two intrepid newsmen. And Ruth Rottecombe had taken to leaving her Volvo estate on the drive near the front door. Added to this the two bull terriers roamed the grounds so that even the usual tradesmen left whatever Mrs Rottecombe had ordered by phone outside the gate where she had to collect it. So she was still there. It was the locked garage doors that held the Superintendent's attention. They suggested that there was something inside that needed to be kept hidden. The Super's intuition told him that it would be as well to have a discreet word with the Chief Constable about the advisability of obtaining a search warrant. The Chief was known to detest the Rottecombes and the case against Battleby had alienated him even further. And since the destruction of their ancestral home and Bob Battleby's arrest for paedophilia there was nothing to fear from the rest of the influential Battlebys. That evening the Superintendent spent an hour with the Chief Constable explaining his suspicions and his dislike of Ruth Rottecombe, and found the Chief shared them.

'This whole thing stinks,' he said. 'That bloody woman's up to her ears in the rotten business but at least we've got that bastard Battleby. And her husband's in deep trouble too, thank goodness. I've had enquiries from . . . well, on high. You might as well say from the office of the Almighty himself, namely the Home Secretary. Take it from me the press coverage isn't doing the Central Office any good. They are as interested in knowing where he's got to as we are and I gained the impression they wouldn't be unhappy if the bastard was dead. Save sacking the blighter.'

By the time the Superintendent left he had been given

permission to apply for a search warrant and to take any reasonable measures he felt like.

One of those measures had been to have the Rottecombes' phone tapped. All he'd learnt was that the wretched Ruth Rottecombe had phoned her husband's flat in London time and time again, and had done the same with his club and the Party Central Office, but no one had seen him.

28

By the time they found Geriatrics 3 – Wilt hadn't been in Geriatrics 5 – Mavis Mottram had had enough. So had Eva. They headed for the door only to be confronted by a formidable Sister.

'I'm sorry but you can't see him yet. Dr Soltander is examining him,' she said.

'But I'm his wife,' squawked Eva.

'Very possibly. But—'

Mavis intervened. 'Show her your driving licence,' she snapped. 'That will prove who you are.' As Eva rummaged in her handbag Mavis turned on the Sister. 'You can check the address. I assume you know Mr Wilt's.'

'Of course we do. We wouldn't know who he was if we didn't.'

'In that case why didn't you phone Mrs Wilt and let her know he was here?'

The Sister gave up and went back into the ward. 'His wife and another dreadful woman are demanding to see him,' she told the doctor.

Dr Soltander sighed. His was a hard life and he had enough terminally ill old people to attend to without having any interruptions from wives and dreadful women. 'Tell them to give me another twenty minutes,' he said. 'I may be in a better position to make a prognosis by then.'

But the Sister wasn't tackling Mavis Mottram again. 'You'd better tell them yourself. They won't listen to me.'

'Very well,' muttered the doctor with a dangerous degree of patience and went out into the corridor. He could see at once what the Sister had meant by 'two dreadful women'. Eva was white-faced and sobbing and demanding to see her Henry. Dr Soltander tried to point out that Wilt was unconscious and in no condition to see anyone and aroused the fury of Mavis Mottram.

'It's her legal right to visit her husband. You can't stop her.'

The doctor's expression hardened. 'And who may you be?'

'Mrs Wilt's friend and I'll repeat that Mrs Wilt has every right to visit her husband.'

Dr Soltander's eyes narrowed. 'Not while I'm doing my rounds,' he snapped. 'She can visit him when I've finished.'

'And when will that be? In four hours?'

'I'm not here to be cross-examined by you or anyone else. Now kindly take your friend into the Waiting Room while I make sure my absence from the ward hasn't resulted in any premature deaths.'

'Presence more likely,' Mavis snapped back and took out her little notebook. 'What's your name? It isn't Shipman by any chance?'

The remark failed to have the effect she had expected. Two effects to be precise. Eva's awful wail startled a number of patients several wards down the corridor and even some on the floor above. At the same time Dr Soltander leant forward with a sinister smile until his face was almost touching Mavis Mottram's.

'Don't tempt me, my dear,' he whispered. 'One day I look forward to having you as a patient.'

And before Mavis could recover from the shock of being nose to nose with such a sinister man he had turned and stalked back into the ward.

'Now if you'll just wait in the Visitors' Room I'll call you just as soon as Dr Soltander is through,' the Sister told them and ushered the two women down the corridor. By the time she returned to the ward the doctor had abandoned Wilt and was taking his fury out on Inspector Flint by explaining that his presence was hindering what little treatment he could give the sick and dying, and that in any case Wilt was not in any condition to be questioned.

'How the devil am I supposed to do the job of three doctors minimum with blasted coppers littering the ward? You can bloody well go and wait with those two diabolical women. Sister, show him out.'

'And my job is to take a statement from this bloke when he comes round,' Flint retorted.

'Yes, well the Sister here will let you know when he does.'

All the same the Inspector wasn't sharing the so-called Visitors' Room with Eva and Mavis Mottram. 'You can phone me at the police station when he's awake,' he told the Sister and went down to the car park. For ten minutes he sat there thinking. Wilt had been found without trousers? And old Mrs Verney had seen him being hoisted out of a car by a woman. And kicked by some drunken louts. It was all very strange.

At Leyline Lodge Ruth Rottecombe was no longer ruthless. She was frantic. The police had arrived early that morning with a search warrant and had insisted she open the garage doors to allow a number of white-coated and gloved forensic experts to make a detailed examination of the place. Still in her dressing gown Ruth had watched them from the kitchen as they moved Harold's Jaguar and then paid particular attention to the patch of oil underneath. Ruth retreated to the bedroom and tried to think. She decided to place the blame on Harold. After all the car was his and he'd obviously done a runner which she could now see was to her advantage. With him out of the way she was still in the clear. After all there was no evidence against her.

She was wrong. In the garage the police had found all the evidence they needed, oil mixed with dried blood, strands of hair and best of all a fragment of blue cloth which matched the colour of the jeans they had found in the lane. There was also mud. They placed all these items in plastic bags and took their findings back to the police station.

'Now we're getting somewhere,' said the Superintendent. 'If this stuff proves to be what it looks like we've got the bitch. Get forensic on to it pronto. And get a match of the cloth with the jeans we found in the lane. If they're the same she's up shit creek without a canoe let alone a paddle. In the mean time see she doesn't leave the house. I want a watch kept on her all the time. And while you're about it bring me the file.'

He sat back and studied his notes from the previous meeting. A bloke named Wilt, Henry Wilt of 45 Oakhurst Avenue, Ipford, found dumped in the street, apparently mugged and now unconscious in hospital there. And the backpacker who'd stayed at the B & Bs had used the same name. All it required was a DNA check on his blood and that found on the floor of the Rottecombes' garage and the case was beginning to build up. The Superintendent gloated at the prospect before him. If he could get the evidence to prove that Ruth the Ruthless was truly involved, however indirectly, in setting the Manor on fire he would earn the gratitude of the Chief Constable who loathed the bitch. And if the Shadow Minister for Social Enhancement was forced to resign or better still was involved himself, his own future looked very bright. He'd be certain of promotion. The Home Secretary would be delighted. The Shadow Minister would certainly lose his seat in the next election and his own future would be assured. The Superintendent stared out the window of his shabby office, then picked up the phone and called Ipford Police Station.

29

In Wilma Auntie Joan wasn't in any mood to gloat. Wally was still in the Coronary Care Unit and she had been assured he would soon recover which was good news. The bad news was that she was met by two men with Yankee accents who insisted she take a look at the pool behind the house.

'Who are you?' she demanded and was shown their IDs which told her they were Federal Drug Enforcement Agents. Auntie Joan wanted to know why they were at the Starfighter Mansion.

'Come on round the back and you'll see why.'

Auntie Joan went reluctantly and was horrified to find the pool empty except for a dead sniffer dog lying on the bottom. Two other men dressed in protective clothing and wearing gas masks were collecting bits of what had once been a gelatine capsule. Not that it was recognisable as such any more.

'Like to tell us just what was hidden down there?' the man named Palowski asked.

Auntie Joan looked wildly at him. 'I don't know what you're talking about.'

'Like the dog drinks the water and the next moment it dies but fast?'

'What's that got to do with me? My husband's in Intensive Care and you're asking me . . . Oh, God!' She turned and headed for the house. She needed a stiff drink and three, at least three, Prozacs and some sleeping pills for good measure. And then the phone rang. She let it. It rang again. And again. Auntie Joanie drank half a tumbler of brandy and took four sleeping tablets. The phone rang another time. She managed to get to it and slurred, 'Fuck off,' and sat down on the floor and passed out.

At Immelmann Enterprises the deputy CEO wished to hell he had taken the day off. His morning had been made hellish. He'd had calls from all over the country from enraged recipients of the quads' emails.

'He called you what?' he asked the first caller, one of IE's biggest customers. 'There's got to have been a mistake. Why would he call you that? He's sick in hospital with a quadruple bypass.'

'And when he comes out he's going to find out just how sick he is. He'll need more than a quadruple bypass by the time I've finished with the cunt-sucker. He wants another million-dollar order from us he ain't going to get it. He gets no more business out of me and what's more I'm taking him to court for defamation. A penis-gobbler, am I? Well, you tell him . . .'

It was a most appalling call. The fifteen others that came in during the rest of the morning weren't any better. Cancellation orders poured in accompanied by physical threats. So did obscene hate emails.

The deputy CEO told the secretary to leave the phone off the hook. 'And while you're about it you'd better be looking for another job. I sure as shit am. Immelmann's gone crazy. He's lost every customer we ever had,' he shouted as he dashed out to his car.

In the Sheriff's office Harry Stallard refused to believe Baxter's report. 'A new sniffer dog died after licking the water in the swimming-pool? Why in the name of God should they empty the pool? The dog probably fell in and drowned.'

But Baxter was adamant. 'There was something dissolved down the bottom and they wanted to see what it was.'

'Sure. One drowned hound dog.'

'All I know is they had special wet suits and masks. And there was this special container to put it in to fly it up to the Chemical Warfare Research Center in Washington for analysis,' Baxter told him. 'They reckon it could be linked to Al Qaeda it's that toxic.'

'In Wilma? In Wilma? That's out-of-this-world crazy. Who the hell's going to use a highly toxic substance in a one-horse town like Wilma?'

Baxter pondered the question. 'Could be that Saddam Hussein bastard. Got to test it someplace, I guess,' he said finally.

'So why choose Wilma he's got all those Kurds he gassed? You tell me that.'

213

'Or that other guy Ossam been . . . The one who did the Twin Towers.'

'Bin Laden,' said the Sheriff. 'Sure. So he chooses Wally Immelmann's swimming-pool and takes out a hound dog? And that makes sense?'

'Shit, I don't know. Nothing makes sense. Hooking the toilets and all up to that tanker back of the old drive-in was crazy.'

Sheriff Stallard pushed his hat back and wiped the sweat from his face. 'I don't believe what I'm hearing. This isn't happening. Not in Wilma it's not. It can't be. Wally Immelmann's in with goddam terrorists. And that ain't possible, no way, Billy, no way. I mean it's way out impossible.'

Baxter shrugged. 'That mega-decibel sound system was impossible too. You heard it. You know.'

The Sheriff did know. He was never going to forget it. He sat thinking. Or trying to. In the end he succeeded and the impossible became slightly more possible and his own position less insecure. People did go loco. 'Get me Maybelle,' he said. 'Bring her in. She's the one who'll know.'

One person who definitely didn't know was Eva. She had finally been allowed out of the Visitors' Room only to be told that the patient Wilt was still unconscious but she could go and see him provided Mavis Mottram didn't accompany her. Having been in Eva Wilt's maudlin company for three hours Mavis had no intention of spending any more time or sympathy on her. She slunk out of the hospital a broken woman, cursing the day she'd met anyone so stupid and mawkishly sentimental. Eva's feelings about Mavis had changed too. She was all bluff and bravado and a bully to boot and had no staying power.

Through the door of the ward Eva had glimpsed Inspector Flint sitting by the bed, apparently reading a newspaper. In fact he wasn't reading it at all; he was using it as a shield to hide what was being done to a man who, if appearances were anything to go by, had recently been trepanned or had had an exceedingly nasty accident with some sort of circular saw. Whatever it was Flint didn't want to see it. He had never been a particularly squeamish man and his experience of mutilated corpses had hardened him to inanimate horrors, but he was less able to cope with those involving modern surgery and in particular found pulsing brains in adult males (babies were different) decidedly unnerving.

'Can't you put a screen round the bed while you're doing whatever you are doing to that poor bloke?' he'd asked only to be told he could leave the ward if he was so wimpish and anyway it wasn't a bloke but a woman and this was a unisex ward.

'You could have fooled me,' Flint retorted. 'Though come to think of it, I daresay unisex is about right. It's impossible to tell what sex anyone is in here.'

It was not a remark that endeared him to three women nearby who had been under the illusion that they were still relatively attractive and sexy. Flint didn't care. He tried to interest himself more vicariously in a scandal involving a well-known rugby player who had gone to a massage parlour in Swansea only to find his wife working there and had tackled the owner or, as the latter had put it from the witness box, 'had gone apeshit', when he saw Wilt looking at him.

Flint put the paper down and smiled. 'Hello, Henry. Feeling any better?'

From the pillow Wilt studied that smile and found it difficult to interpret. It wasn't the sort of smile to give him any confidence. Inspector Flint's false teeth were too loose for that and besides, he had seen Flint smile maliciously in the past too often to find the sight at all reassuring. He didn't feel any better.

'Better than what?' he asked.

Flint's smile disappeared and with it most of his sympathy. He began to doubt whether Wilt's brain had been affected at all by being mugged. 'Well, better than you did before.'

'Before what?' said Wilt, fighting for time to find out what was going on. It was obvious he was in hospital and that he had bandages round his head but that was about all that was obvious.

Flint's hesitation before replying did nothing to give him any confidence in his own innocence. 'Before this thing happened,' he said finally.

Wilt tried to think. He had no idea what had happened. 'I can't say I do,' he replied. It seemed a reasonable answer to a question he didn't understand.

That wasn't the way Inspector Flint saw it. He was already beginning to lose the thread of the conversation and as always with Wilt he was being led into a swamp of misunderstanding. The sod never did say anything that was at all clear-cut. 'When you say you can't say you do, just exactly what do you mean?' he enquired and tried to smile again. That didn't help.

Wilt's caution went into overdrive. 'Just that,' he said.

'And "just that" means?'

'What I said. Just that,' Wilt said.

Again Flint's smile vanished. He leant forward. 'Listen, Henry, all I want to know is—'

He got no further. Wilt had decided on new avoiding tactics. 'Who's Henry?' he asked abruptly.

A new look of doubt came on Flint's face and his lean forward ground to a halt. 'Who's Henry? You want to know who Henry is?'

'Yes. I don't know of any Henrys. Except kings and princes of course and I wouldn't know any of them, would I? Never met one and I'm not likely to. Have you ever met a king or a prince?'

For a second the look on the Inspector's face had changed from doubt to certainty. Now it swung back again. With Wilt nothing was certain and even that was doubtful in these circumstances. Wilt was uncertainty personified. 'No. I haven't met a king or a prince and I don't want to. All I want to know—'

'That's the second time you've said that,' said Wilt. 'And what I want to know is who I am.'

At that moment Eva shoved her way into the room. She had waited long enough and she wasn't spending another two hours in that revoltingly dirty waiting room. She was going to her husband's side.

'Oh, darling, are you in terrible pain, my pet?'

Wilt opened his eyes with a silent curse. 'What's it got to do with you? And who are you calling "darling"?'

'But . . . oh, God! I'm your Eva, your wife.'

'Wife? What do you mean? I haven't got a wife,' Wilt moaned. 'I'm a . . . I'm a . . . I don't know what I am.'

In the background Inspector Flint agreed whole-heartedly. He didn't know what Wilt was either. Never had and never would. About the nearest he'd ever got to it was that Wilt was the most devious bastard he'd come across in all the years he'd been in the police force. With Eva, now weeping copiously, you knew precisely where you stood. Or lay. At the bottom of the pile. To that extent Wilt had told the truth. Family first with those ghastly quads; Eva second, along with her material possessions – or, as Wilt's solicitor had once put it, 'like living with a dishwasher cum vacuum cleaner that thinks it thinks' – and finally whatever latest fad or so-called philosophical twaddle she had heard about. Even Greenpeace had found her militancy too much. The Keeper of the Seal Culling Station at Worthcombe Bay had, in giving evidence in court against her from his wheelchair, said that if she represented Greenpeace, he shuddered to think what Greenwar would be like. In fact the man's language had been so filthy that only his injuries prevented the magistrate from holding him in contempt. And finally at the very bottom of the pile was Mr Henry Wilt, lawfully wedded husband of Mrs Eva Wilt, poor bugger. No wonder he deliberately refused to recognise her.

He was distracted from these considerations by one last desperate appeal from Eva to her Henry to acknowledge her as his devoted wife and mother of his lovely daughters, and Wilt's refusal to do anything so utterly insane, as well as his complaint that he was sick and didn't want to be harassed by strange women he'd never seen before. The effect of this statement was that the weeping Eva was helped from the ward. Her sobs could be heard from the corridor as she went in search of a doctor.

Inspector Flint seized the opportunity to go back to the bedside and bend over Wilt. 'You're a cunning bugger, Henry,' he whispered. 'Cunning as hell but you don't fool me. I saw the nasty little glint in your eye when your missis took off. I've known you too long to be fooled by your tricks. You just remember that.'

For a moment he thought Wilt was about to smile but the gormless expression returned and Wilt closed his eyes. Flint gave up. He wasn't going to get anything useful out of him in these awful circumstances. And the circumstances were getting more awful by the minute. The woman with the pulsating skull was having some sort of fit and one of the shaven multi-sexes was protesting to a nurse that he, she or it had already been given a forty-five-minutes oil enema and definitely didn't need another. The whole thing was a bloody nightmare.

In Wilma Sheriff Stallard shared Inspector Flint's horror though for very different reasons. It wasn't so much that Maybelle was refusing to give him information about what had been going on at the Starfighter Mansion. She was giving far too much and he'd have preferred not to hear it.

'They asked you what?' he gasped when she told him the quads had asked her how many times a week Wally Immelmann fucked her and how many other gays there were in Wilma. 'The filthy bitches. And they used the words "fucked" and "asswise"?'

Maybelle nodded. 'Yessir, they sure did.'

'What in God's name did they ask that for? It's crazy. It's not possible.'

'Said they were doing a project on exploitation of coloured folk in the South for the school they go to back in Britain and they had to fill in a questionnaire,' Maybelle said.

'And what did you tell them, for Chrissake?'

'I'd rather not say, Sheriff. Nothing more than the truth.'

The Sheriff shuddered. If the truth was anything like what he'd heard at a thousand decibels up near the lake,

Wally Immelmann would have to get the hell out of Wilma but fast. Either that or be lucky to die in the Coronary Unit.

30

Two days later Wilt was sitting in a chair explaining what it felt like not to know who he was to a doctor who seemed to find Wilt's symptoms quite common and of rather less interest than Wilt himself.

'And you really don't know who you are? Are you quite sure about that?' the psychiatrist asked for the fifth time. 'Are you absolutely certain?'

Wilt considered the question very carefully. It wasn't so much the question as the way it was put that concerned him. It had a familiar tone to it. In his years of teaching confirmed and convincing liars he had used that tone himself too often not to recognise what it meant. Wilt changed his tactics.

'Do you know who you are?' he asked.

'As a matter of fact, I do. My name is Dr Dedge.'

'That's not what I meant,' said Wilt. 'That is your identity. But do you know who you are?'

Dr Dedge regarded him with a new interest. Patients who distinguished between personal identity and who they were came into a rather different category from his usual ones. On the other hand, the fact that Wilt's notes mentioned 'Police inquiries following head injuries' still inclined him to believe he was feigning amnesia. Dr Dedge took up the challenge.

'When you say "who you are" what exactly do you mean? "Who" surely implies personal identity, doesn't it?'

'No,' said Wilt. 'I know perfectly well that I am Henry Wilt of 45 Oakhurst Avenue. That is my identity and my address. What I want to know is who Henry Wilt is.'

'You don't know who Henry Wilt is?'

'Of course I don't, any more than I know how I came to be in the ward.'

'It says here that you suffered head injuries—'

'I know that,' Wilt interrupted. 'I've got bandages round my head. Not that that is proof positive but even the most overworked NHS doctor would hardly make the mistake of treating my head when I'd broken my ankle. At least I don't suppose so. Of course anything is possible these days. On the other hand, who I am is still a mystery to me. Are you sure you really know who you are, Dr Dredger?'

The psychiatrist smiled professionally. 'My name happens to be Dedge, not Dredger.'

'Well, mine is Wilt and I still don't know who I am.'

Dr Dedge decided to go back to the safer ground of clinical questions. 'Do you remember what you were doing when this neurological insult occurred?' he asked.

'Not offhand I don't,' said Wilt, after a moment's hesitation. 'When would that be, this neurological insult?'

'When you suffered the head injuries.'

'Bit more of an insult being beaten over the head, I'd have thought. Still, if that's what you call it . . .'

'That is the technical term for what occurred to you, Mr Wilt. Now do you know what you were doing just before the incident?'

Wilt pretended to think about the question. Not that it needed much thinking about. He had no idea. 'No,' he said finally.

'No? Nothing at all?'

Wilt shook his head carefully. 'Well, I can remember watching the news and thinking how wrong it was to stop Meals on Wheel to those old people in Burling just to save on the Council Tax. Then Eva – that's my wife – came in and said supper was ready. I can't remember much after that. Oh, and I washed the car some time and the cat had to go to the vet again. I can't remember much after that.'

The psychiatrist made a number of notes and nodded encouragingly. 'Any little thing will be of help, Henry,' he said. 'Take your time.'

Wilt did. He needed to find out how far back his memory would have been affected by a neurological insult. He'd nearly fallen into a trap when he'd said he didn't know his own name. Clearly that didn't fit the pattern. Not knowing who he was, on the other hand, still had some mileage to it. Wilt tried again.

'I remember . . . no, you wouldn't be interested in that.'

'Let me be the one who decides that, Henry. You just tell me what you remember.'

'I can't, Doctor, I mean . . . well . . . I just can't,' he said, adopting the shifty whine he had heard so often in the Disadvantaged Single Sex Seminars he had been forced to attend as part of Ms Lashskirt's Gender Affirmation Awareness Programme. Wilt was using that whine to his own advantage now.

In front of him Dr Dedge softened noticeably. He felt safer with that whine. It smacked of dependence. 'I'm interested in anything you have to say,' he said.

Wilt doubted it. What Dr Dedge was interested in was finding out if he was shamming. 'Well, it's just that I'm sitting in this room and suddenly I feel like I don't know why I'm here or who I am. It doesn't make sense. Sounds so silly, doesn't it?'

'No, not at all. This is a not uncommon occurrence. Does this sensation last long?'

'I don't know, Doctor. I can't remember. I just know I have it and it doesn't make any sense.'

'And have you discussed it with your wife?' Dr Dedge asked.

'Well, no. Can't say I have,' said Wilt sheepishly. 'I mean, she's got enough on her plate without me not knowing who I am. What with the quads and all.'

'Mrs Wilt . . .? Are you telling me you have quadruplets?' asked the psychiatrist.

Wilt gave a sickly smile. 'Yes, Doctor, four of them. All girls. And even the cat's neutered. Got no tail either. So I just sit there and try to think who I am.'

By the time Wilt went back to the ward, Dr Dedge had

no doubt that he was a deeply disturbed man. As he explained to Dr Soltander, the neurological insult had resulted in the emergence of partial amnesia as a complicating factor to a pre-existing depressive condition. And a bed had become available in an isolation room because the previous patient, a youth on a drug charge, had hanged himself. Dr Soltander was glad to hear it. He had had enough of Wilt and more importantly he had had far more than enough of Mrs Wilt who had been besieging his ward and disturbing the terminally ill patients.

'Best place for him and those bloody policemen.'

'He's in Psychiatry, is he? Well, I can't say I'm surprised,' Inspector Flint said when he found Wilt was no longer in Geriatrics 3 next day. 'If you ask me, he should have been certified years ago when he stuffed that inflatable doll down the hole. All the same, I don't think he's half as sick as he's making out. I think he's holding something back. I didn't like the way he was acting when I was there.'

'In what way, sir?' Sergeant Yates asked.

'Pretending he doesn't know who he is and he's never seen me in his life. Bullshit, Yates, pure Grade A unadulterated bullshit. And he doesn't know Eva Wilt either? My eye and Betty Martin he doesn't. He could have had half his brain removed and he'd still remember her. Mrs Wilt isn't someone even a brain-damaged coma case would be capable of forgetting. No, our Henry was having her on. And me. Why, Yates, why? You tell me.'

But the Sergeant couldn't. He was still having trouble with that 'brain-damaged coma case' and trying to work out how one could be in a coma without having some sort of brain damage. Didn't make sense. But then half the things Inspector Flint said these days didn't make sense to Sergeant Yates. Must be getting old or something.

'Any new suspects out at New Estate?'

The Sergeant shook his head. 'The place is loaded with junkies and hooligans. All those empty tower blocks. It would take a week or more to search them all. Anyway, they could have moved on somewhere else.'

'True,' said Flint and sighed. 'Probably stoned out of their minds and don't even remember doing him over. What beats me is why he wasn't wearing trousers.'

'Could be he was looking for a bit of—' Yates began.

The Inspector stopped him. 'If you're suggesting Wilt's gay, don't. Not that I'd blame him if he was with a wife like Eva. Can't be much fun having it off with a woman that size. We've checked with the staff at the Tech and, if what I've heard is true, he's reckoned to be practically a homophobe. No, you can forget that idea. There's something weird about this case. Anyway, that phone call from Oston gives us a line on what he's been up to. I got the impression that this case isn't a simple case of our Wilty being mugged. That Super spoke about Scotland Yard being called in which means they've got bigger fish to fry. Much bigger fish.'

'Torching a manor house is big enough. I know Wilt's not right in the head but I can't see him doing that.'

'He didn't. That's out of the question. Wilt wouldn't know how to light a bonfire let alone a bloody great house. That's definitely not on. And as for leaving his gear behind too. Not even Wilt would do that. Still, it does give us some sort of lead on where he's been.'

The phone rang again in the next office. 'It's for you,' Yates told him.

Flint went through and took it. Ten minutes later he returned with a smile. 'Looks as if we're off the case. They're sending two CID men up from London to interrogate our Mr Wilt. I wish them luck. They going to need it if they think they can get any information out of the lunatic.'

31

'This blasted business is getting out of hand,' the Chief
Constable told the Superintendent at Oston. He'd driven
over in his wife's small car to convey this message
unostentatiously. The disappearance of the Shadow
Minister for Social Enhancement had aggravated an
already difficult situation. The media had returned in
force and were encamped outside Leyline Lodge in even
larger numbers than before. 'I've had the Home Secretary
on the line asking where the precious Shadow Minister
has got to and the Shadow Cabinet are practically
hysterical at the adverse publicity they are getting. First
Battleby and the arson and paedophile charges, then the
ghastly woman with those damned bull terriers and now
that idiot Rottecombe's disappeared. They're sending
someone up from Scotland Yard or MI5. I have an idea
there's something else. Has to do with the Americans but
hopefully it's not our pigeon. Now then, I want those
media blighters out of the way when you pick her up. But
it's got to be done tactfully. Any ideas?'

The Superintendent tried to think. 'I suppose we could
create some sort of diversion and get them away from the
house for a time,' he said finally. 'It would have to be
something pretty sensational. Ruth the Ruthless is the

one they're after. And I can't say I blame them. She'll make good headlines.'

They sat in silence for a few minutes, the Chief Constable considering the damage the wretched Shadow Minister for Social Enhancement and his sadistic wife had inflicted on the county.

The Superintendent was more preoccupied with his idea of a diversion. 'If only some lunatics would let off a bomb. The Real IRA would be perfect. The media horde would be off like a shot . . .'

The Chief Constable shook his head. One gaggle of media hounds was bad enough, a second swarming over the place would only bring more awful publicity. 'I can't take responsibility for anything like that. Besides, where the hell could you get a bomb? You've got to come up with something less complicated.'

'I suppose so. I'll let you know,' he told the Chief Constable who'd got up to go.

'What we don't want is anything that's sensational. You understand that?'

The Superintendent said he did. He sat on in his office thinking dark thoughts and cursing the Rottecombes. An hour later a Woman Police Sergeant came in and asked if he'd like a cup of coffee. She was slim and fair-haired and had good legs. By the time she'd fetched the stuff they called coffee he'd made up his mind. He crossed the room and locked the door.

'Take a seat, Helen,' he said. 'I've got a job for you. You don't have to take it but . . .'

By the time he had finished the Sergeant had reluctantly agreed. 'What about those two bull terriers? I mean, I don't want to be torn to bits by them. What they did to those two reporters wasn't funny.'

'We'll have taken care of them. Dropped some doped meat into the garden from a helicopter. They'll be snoring their heads off in no time at all.'

'I certainly hope so,' said the Sergeant.

'We'll go in this evening when those fellows down by the gate are taking it in turns to go to the pub.'

Inside Leyline Lodge Ruth Rottecombe was expecting the raid. She'd been phoned a number of times by the police asking her to go to Oston to answer some more questions and had, after the first call, simply not bothered to answer the phone. She took only those she could identify on the LCD panel. She'd also been bothered by a great many calls from the Central Office demanding to know where the Shadow Minister for Social Enhancement had got to.

For a moment Ruth was tempted to say he was probably holed up with a rent-boy but Harold still had his uses if only she could find him. The journalists besieging the Lodge made it impossible to leave the house. She'd been up to the skylight to check and had seen something else that scared her. Two uniformed policemen in the field across the old stone wall. They weren't hiding, either, just making it obvious she was under surveillance. But why? It had to be something to do with what the forensic men had found on the floor of the garage and taken away in plastic bags. That was the only explanation she could think of. Bloodstained earth from the man's head wound. That had to be the answer. She cursed herself for not having scrubbed the floor. As the sun began to sink in the West Ruth the Ruthless sat in her husband's study and tried to think what to do. About the only thing she could come up with was to lay the blame on Harold. After all, his Jaguar had been parked over the patch of oil and blood and there was nothing to indicate she had moved it there.

She'd just reached this conclusion when she heard the sound of a vehicle coming up the drive. It wasn't the usual police car but an ambulance. What the hell was an ambulance doing outside the house? And where on earth were Wilfred and Pickles? They usually went into the hall when a car arrived. She found them in their baskets in the kitchen, fast asleep. She prodded them with her foot but they didn't stir. That was strange but before she could do anything to wake them the ambulance had turned in the driveway and had backed up to the front door. For a brief moment Ruth Rottecombe thought they must have found Harold. She opened the door and a moment later had been hustled into the back of the ambulance by two hefty policewomen dressed as nurses and was being held face down on a stretcher. Four constables had entered the house only to return carrying the bull terriers, still sound asleep in their baskets. They joined her on the floor. Ruth tried to turn her head but failed.

'Where are the keys of the Volvo?' a woman asked.

'Don't know,' Ruth tried to scream but her face was pressed against the canvas and her words were muffled.

'What she say?'

For a moment they lifted her head and this time Ruth called them fucking bitches before being shoved down again.

'Don't worry. I'll find them,' the Woman Sergeant called Helen said and got on the walkie-talkie. 'Just see you open the gate when I come down in the Volvo and clear that mob out of the way. I'll be moving fast.'

As the rear doors of the ambulance were slammed shut she went into the house and the ambulance drove off at high speed. Ten minutes later she emerged wearing Ruth Rottecombe's skirt and twin set. She had the keys of the Volvo and was driving very fast when she swung through the open gate, nearly taking a reporter with her. As he leapt to one side she turned to the left at speed and took a side road to Oston.

'Which hospital they going to?' a cameraman who had taken refuge in the hedge asked one of the cops on the gate.

'Blocester, I'd say. That's where emergency cases go. Wouldn't be anywhere else. You turn right on the main road,' he said and padlocked the gate. The media mob ran for their cars and set off in pursuit. The leading car was stopped by a patrol car a mile further on and the driver was threatened with dangerous driving. Behind it the other cars skidded to a halt. A mile ahead the ambulance turned left, slowed down and waited in a lay-by for the

Volvo. By the time the reporters' cars reached the T-junction and were heading for Blocester, Ruth Rottecombe had been transferred to the Volvo. And at Oston Police Station she was taken through to a cell that had been occupied by a drunk who had puked the previous night. It still stank of vomit. Ruth had slumped on to the metal bed bolted to the floor and with her head between her hands was staring at the floor. Outside, the empty ambulance had turned and was moving at normal speed towards Blocester. After three hours she was escorted to the Superintendent's office, demanding to know why she had been treated in this outrageous fashion and promising her husband would be making official complaint to the Home Secretary.

'That's going to be a little difficult,' came the answer. 'You want to know why?'

Ruth Rottecombe did.

'Because he's dead. We've found his body and it looks very much as though he was murdered.' He paused to let this news sink in. As Ruth sagged in her chair and was apparently going to faint he went on. 'Take her back to her cell. She's had a tiring day. We'll question her in the morning.' There was no sympathy in his voice.

32

Flint's hopes that the two men from London would take him off the case had been dashed. In the first place they weren't from Scotland Yard or, if they were, the shortage of officers in London was even more desperate than he'd supposed. The Metropolitan Police had to be recruiting abroad, in this case in America. That was his first impression when they entered his office with Hodge grinning in the background. The impression didn't last. The two Americans sat down unasked and stared at Flint for a moment. They evidently didn't like what they were seeing.

'You Inspector Flint?' the bigger of the two asked.

'I am,' said Flint. 'And who may you be?'

They looked disparagingly round the office before answering. 'American Embassy. Undercover,' they said in unison and flashed ID cards so briefly Flint couldn't read them.

'We understand you've been interrogating a suspect called Wilt,' the thinner man said.

But Flint had been riled. He was damned if he was going to be questioned by two Americans who wouldn't identify themselves politely. Not with Hodge gloating in the background.

'You can understand what you like,' he said grimly and glared at Hodge. 'Ask him. He's the person who thinks he knows.'

'He's told us. The Superintendent has been very cooperative.'

It was on the tip of Flint's tongue to say Hodge's cooperation wasn't worth a fly's fart but he restrained himself. If these arrogant bastards wanted to pin a drug-dealing charge on Henry Wilt he was going to let them walk into the morass of misunderstanding the moronic Hodge would provide. He had better things to do. Like find out why Wilt had been assaulted and found half-naked in the New Estate.

He got up and walked past the two Americans. 'If you want any information I'm sure the Super will give it to you,' he said as he opened the door. 'He's the drugs expert.'

He went out and down to the canteen and had a cup of tea overlooking the car park. Presently Hodge and the two men came into view and climbed into a car with darkened windows parked next to his own. Flint moved back to another table where he could see them but remain out of sight himself. After five minutes the car was still there. The Inspector gave them another ten. No movement. So they were waiting to see where he went. The buggers could sit there all bloody day. He got up, went downstairs and out the front door and walked to the bus station and caught a bus going to the hospital. He sat at the back in a thoroughly belligerent mood.

'Anyone would think this was Iraq,' he muttered to himself and was assured by an intense woman in the next seat that it wasn't and was he all right?

'Schizophrenia,' he said and looked at her in a distinctly sinister manner. The woman got off at the next stop and Flint felt better. He'd learnt something from Henry Wilt after all: the gift of confusing people.

By the time he reached the hospital and the bus turned round he'd begun to devise his new tactics. Hodge and those two arrogant Yanks would be bound to go up to 45 Oakhurst Avenue and ask Eva or, if she wasn't there, the quads, where Wilty was and as sure as eggs were eggs she'd say, 'At the hospital.' Flint went into the empty bus shelter and took out his mobile and dialled the number he knew so well.

Eva answered.

Flint put his handkerchief over the mouthpiece and assumed what he hoped was a high-pitched la-di-da voice. 'Is that Mrs Wilt?' he asked.

Eva said it was.

'I'm calling from the Methuen Mental Hospital. I'm sorry to have to tell you that your husband Mr Henry Wilt has been transferred to the Serious Head Injuries Unit for an exploratory operation and—' He got no further. Eva gave an awful wail. Flint waited a moment and then went on.

'I'm afraid he's in no condition to have any visitors for the next three days. We'll keep you informed of his progress. I repeat, he's to have no visitors no matter who they are. Please ensure he is not disturbed by anyone. We are particularly anxious no attempt is made by the police to question him. He's in no condition to be put under any pressure. Is that clear?'

It was an unnecessary question. Eva was sobbing noisily and in the background the quads were asking what the matter was. Flint cut the mobile off and went up to the hospital with a smile on his face. If Hodge and those two American goons turned up at Oakhurst Avenue they'd get a rough ride from Eva Wilt.

What Ruth Rottecombe was getting was a very rough ride indeed. Now that Harold's battered body had been found still being buffeted by the waves on the rocks of the North Cornish coast near Morwenstow, and the local doctor's original finding that the blow on his head had been inflicted before he drowned had been confirmed by a forensic expert helicoptered down from London, the police were taking a serious view of his death.

So were the Special Branch men sent down to assist the local police at Oston. They were particularly interested in the connecting evidence that the blood of the man named Wilt found on the New Estate in Ipford matched that on cloth found in the garage at Leyline Lodge and on the jeans Ruth had dumped in the lane behind Meldrum Manor. Worst of all from Ruth's point of view was the fact that the number-plate of her Volvo estate had been recorded by a motorway camera as she'd driven back from the New Estate at nearly 100 m.p.h. in an attempt to get home before dawn. The finding of Wilt's knapsack in the attic added to the evidence against her. For the first time she wished to hell Harold hadn't been Shadow Minister for Social Enhancement. That fact made the police investigation very high priority indeed. Shadow Ministers who died in suspicious, very suspicious, circumstances meant that the rules of interrogation could be stretched. And to avoid any further intrusions by the media she had been moved from Oston to Rossdale.

At the same time the police methodically searched Leyline Lodge and took away a number of canes and any heavier objects which could have been used to inflict the head wound on Harold Rottecombe's head before he had, as they imagined, been pushed unconscious into the river. Urged on by the Party Central Committee officials they dismissed the possibility that the Shadow Minister's death had been accidental.

'He drowned in the river and that's for sure,' the senior CID Inspector told the police group dealing with the case. 'Forensic checked the water in his lungs and it wasn't sea water. They're absolutely definite about that. They can't be certain of the date he died but it was almost certainly a week to ten days ago. Probably more. That's one thing we know. Secondly, his Jag is still in the garage so he didn't drive down to the coast and chuck himself off the cliffs. That goes without saying. Another thing, his wife had driven the car or moved it at any rate because her fingerprints were on the steering-wheel, weren't they?'

The Superintendent from Oston confirmed this. 'They indicated she was the last person to use the car,' he said.

Then there was the blood on the floor of the Volvo estate where Wilt had bled. 'Which confirms what she was doing in Ipford. So we've got her on any number of charges, and more importantly this bloke Wilt had the same type of head wound as her husband. So we go on questioning her round the clock until she breaks. Oh, and one other thing, we've been looking into her background and it stinks. False birth certificate, prostitute specialising in S & M, she's done the lot. As hard as they come.'

'Hasn't she asked to phone her lawyer?' another detective asked.

The CID Chief Inspector smiled. 'Phoned her husband's lawyer and strangely enough he's not available. Says he's on holiday. Well, that's what he's told me. Gone to France. Very wise of him. She can have legal aid, of course. Some dimmy who'll do her more harm than good and she knows it so she's refused.'

In the Interrogation Room Ruth the Ruthless was refusing to answer questions too.

33

As Flint had hoped the arrival of Hodge and the two Americans at 45 Oakhurst Avenue was not a success. They found Eva in tears.

'I don't know where he is,' she sobbed. 'He's just disappeared. We came back from America and found he'd gone but I don't know where. There was no note or anything and his credit cards were on the kitchen table, and his chequebook. He hadn't taken any money out of the bank so I don't know what to think.'

'Could be he's had an accident. Have you tried the hospital?'

'Of course I have. The first thing I did but they were no help.'

'Has he shown any interest in any other women?' one of the Americans asked, regarding her critically.

Eva's tears stopped immediately. She had had enough of Americans and particularly plainclothes police ones who wore shades and drove up in cars with darkened windows.

'No, he hasn't,' she snapped. 'He's always been a very good husband so you can go to hell, asking questions like that.'

On this furious note she slammed the door in their

faces. They went back to the car and discovered they had a flat. From the upstairs window of their room the quads watched gleefully. Josephine had let the tyre down.

At the hospital Inspector Flint was surprised to be met in the corridor by Dr Dedge. The psychiatrist was looking desperately haggard and kept shaking his head in a helpless sort of manner.

'Thank God you've come,' he said, and grasping Flint's arm he dragged him into his office, indicated a chair and slumped into one behind his desk. He opened a drawer and took several blue pills.

'Having a difficult time with our friend Wilt?' Flint asked.

The doctor stared at him with bulging eyes. 'Difficult?' he gasped incredulously. 'Difficult? That bastard in there had the gall to get me out of bed at 4 a.m. this morning to tell me I was descended from the Pongid family.' He paused to get a glass of water and another blue pill.

'You mean to say you drove back here—' Flint began but Dr Dedge seemed to be having a choking fit.

'Drove? I didn't drive. I'm forced to sleep in here on that bloody couch in the corner in case yet another lunatic chooses to hang himself or go berserk in the night. That's how short-staffed we are. And I'm a highly qualified psychiatrist specialising in serious cases of paranoid psychotic disorder, not a damned night-watchman.'

Flint was about to say he sympathised when the doctor went on.

'And to cap it all that swine in there sleeps all day and seems to spend all night devising fiendish questions for me and ringing the panic button. You don't know what he's like.'

Flint said he did. 'He's the master of inconsequential answers. I've questioned him for hours on end and he always goes off at a tangent.'

Dr Dedge leant forward on to his desk. 'I'm not asking him questions. The bastard's asking me. At 4 a.m. he asked me if I realised I was 99.4 per cent a baboon because that's what DNA analysis indicated. That's what he meant by my ancestral family being members of the Pongid family.'

'Actually he's got it wrong. He didn't mean baboon. He was talking about chimpanzees,' said Flint in an effort to calm the man down.

It didn't work. Dr Dedge looked wildly at him. 'A chimpanzee? Are you mad too? Do I look like a baboon or a chimpanzee and I've never had a DNA analysis and what's with my ancestors being Pongids? My father was a Dedge and my mother's family name is Fawcett and always has been since 1605. We've done a genealogical tree on both sides of the family and there's no one called Pongid on it.'

Inspector Flint tried another tack. 'He's been reading the papers. There's been all this stuff about Pongids being older than Hominids and *Homo sapiens*. The latest theory is—'

'Fuck the latest theory!' shouted the psychiatrist. 'I

want some sleep. Can't you take that maniac off to the police station and give him the third degree there?'

'No,' said Flint firmly. 'He's a sick man and—'

'You can say that again and I'm going to join him if he stays here much longer. Anyway, we've done scans and all the tests needed and they none of them indicate any actual damage to his brain – if that's what's inside his blasted head.'

Flint sighed and went out into the corridor and entered the Isolation Room to find Wilt sitting up in bed smiling to himself. He'd rather enjoyed what he'd heard the doctor shouting next door. The Inspector stood at the end of the bed and stared at Wilt for a moment. Whatever he'd done to drive Dr Dedge virtually out of his mind it was clear to Flint that Wilt had all or most of his senses about him. He decided his tactics. He'd had a long conversation on the phone with the Superintendent in Oston and knew where Wilt had been. Two could play a game of bluff.

'All right, Henry,' he said and took out a pair of handcuffs. 'This time you've gone too far. Faking the murder of your missis by dumping an inflatable doll dressed in her clothes down a pile hole when you knew perfectly well she was alive and on a stolen boat with those Californians was one thing, but arson and the murder of a Shadow Minister is another. So you can wipe that smile off your face.'

Wilt's smile vanished.

Flint locked the door and sat down very close to the bed.

'Murder? Murder of a Shadow Minister?' said Wilt, now genuinely startled.

'You heard me. Murder and arson in a village called Meldrum Slocum.'

'Meldrum Slocum? I've never even heard of the place.'

'Then you tell me how your jeans were found in a lane behind the Manor House there which some bastard torched. Your jeans, Henry, with burn marks and ash on them and you've never heard of the place. Don't give me that bullshit.'

'But I swear to God—'

'You can swear all you like but the evidence is there. First, the jeans with mud on them found in a lane behind the burnt-out house. And the mud matches that in the lane. Third, you were definitely in the garage belonging to the murdered Shadow Minister. They've done a DNA test on that blood and it fits yours exactly. They also found your knapsack inside the house of the other suspect. These are the facts. Undeniable facts. And just to cheer you up let me tell you Scotland Yard are involved. This is not something you can talk your way out of this time like you've done before.'

Flint let this awful information sink into Wilt's bewildered mind. He tried to remember how all this had happened but only disjointed scenes came back to him.

'Think, Henry, think. This isn't some prank. I'm telling you the gospel truth.'

Wilt looked at him and knew that Inspector Flint was deadly serious.

'I don't know what happened to me and that's the gospel truth too. I remember not wanting to go to America to stay with Eva's Aunt Joan and her husband Wally Immelmann. So I told her I had a class to prepare for next term and got some books Wally Immelmann would hate out of the library and of course she made a fuss and said I couldn't take them.'

'What sort of books?'

'Oh, books about Castro's wonderful Cuba and the Marxist Theory of Revolution. The sort of stuff he detests. I can't say I like it myself but he'd have had an apoplectic fit if I'd turned up in Wilma with the books I said I was going to take. There were others but I can't remember them all.'

'And your missis swallowed that story?'

'Hook, line and sinker,' said Wilt. 'Anyway, it was plausible. We've still got lunatics who think Lenin was a saint and Stalin was fundamentally a kindly chap at heart. Some people never learn, do they?'

Flint kept his thoughts on the matter to himself. 'All right, I'll accept what you've told me so far. What I want to know is what you did next. And don't give me any hogwash about having amnesia. The doctors say your brain hasn't been damaged. At least not any more than it was before you got into this scrape.'

'I can tell you what I did up to a certain point but after that until I woke up in that Terminal Ward I haven't a clue. The last thing I remember was being in a wood soaked to the skin and stumbling forward over a root or something and falling. From then on, nothing. I can't help you any further.'

'OK, let's go back a bit. Where had you come from?' said the Inspector.

'That's the point. I don't know. I was on a walking tour.'

'From where to where?'

'I didn't know. In fact I didn't want to know. I just wanted to go nowhere. You see what I mean?'

Flint shook his head. 'Not one bloody word,' he said. 'You didn't want to know. You just wanted to go. And that makes sense? Not to me it doesn't. A lot of gibberish is what it sounds like to me. Deliberate gibberish. Like lies. You had to know where you wanted to go.'

Wilt sighed. He'd known Inspector Flint on and off for a good number of years and he should have predicted the Inspector wouldn't understand that he didn't want to know where he was going. He tried to explain again.

'I wanted to get away from Ipford, the Tech, the routine of going to work, if you can call it work, and clear my mind of all that junk by finding England without any preconceptions.'

Flint tried to grasp what Wilt was saying and failed as usual. 'So how come you ended up in Meldrum Slocum?' he said in a desperate attempt to get some sanity into the conversation. 'You must have come from somewhere.'

'I told you. From a wood. And anyhow I was pissed.'

'And I'm pissed off with having the mickey taken out

of me,' snarled Flint and went back to Dr Dedge's office and banged on the door only to be told to fuck off.

'All I want to know is if that bloody man is well enough to go home. Just tell me that.'

'Listen!' shouted the psychiatrist. 'I don't give a damn whether he is well or not. Get him out of here. He'll be the death of me. Is that good enough for you?'

'Would you say he ought to be in a mental hospital?' asked Flint.

'I can't think of a better place for the swine!' yelled Dr Dedge.

'In that case I'll need you to certify him.'

He was answered by a moan. 'I can't do that. He's not certifiably insane,' the psychiatrist said and opened the door. He was in his underpants. He hesitated for a moment and came to a decision. 'I tell you what I will do. I'll recommend him for assessment and leave the doctors at the Methuen to make the decision.'

And on this note he crossed to his desk and filled in a form and handed it to the Inspector. 'That will get him off my back at any rate.'

Flint went back to Wilt. 'You heard what he said. You don't have to stay here any longer.'

'What did he mean by assessment?'

'Don't ask me. I'm not a psychiatrist,' said the Inspector.

'Nor is he, come to that,' said Wilt but he got out of bed and began looking for his clothes. There weren't any. 'I'm not going anywhere dressed like this,' he said, indicating the long nightdress he'd been given in the Geriatric Ward.

Flint went back to Dr Dedge whose temper hadn't improved. 'In the clothes he came in, of course,' he snarled through the door.

'But they were taken away as evidence that he'd been assaulted.'

'Try the Morgue. There's bound to be a corpse down there with clothes his size. Now leave me alone to get some sleep.'

The Inspector went down the corridor, asked directions to the Morgue and, having finally found it and explained his reason for coming, was called a grave robber and told to get the hell out. In a fury he went back and snitched a white coat from a male nurse's dressing room when its owner was in the lavatory. Ten minutes later Wilt, dressed in the white coat which was far too short to cover his hospital gown, was in the bus with Flint, on his way to the Methuen Mental Hospital protesting vehemently that he didn't need 'assessing'.

'All they'll do is ask you a few simple questions and let you go,' Flint told him. 'Anyway, it's a damned sight better than being sectioned.'

'And what precisely does that mean?' Wilt asked.

'Being declared insane and held against your will.'

Wilt said nothing. He'd changed his mind about being assessed.

34

In Wilma the Drug Enforcement Agents had given up their surveillance of the Starfighter Mansion. An autopsy of the sniffer dog and the analysis of the remains of the capsule on the bottom of the pool had indicated nothing in the least suspicious. The dog had died of natural causes almost certainly brought on by a lifetime's diet of drugs to give him the nose for heroin, crack cocaine, ecstasy, opium, LSD, marijuana and anything else that came on the market. In short the dog was a raving drug addict and recently it had been forced to inhale tobacco smoke, the latest banned substance, to such an extent that shortly before its death it had eaten two cigarette butts in a desperate effort to assuage this new addiction. All in all it had been a thoroughly sick dog.

The same could not be said for the water in the pool. It had recently been emptied and refilled and there were no traces of illegal substances in the one hundred thousand gallons of fresh water.

'You should have hooked the pool outlet up to the analyser tank back of the old drive-in,' Murphy told the men who had been checking what came out of the toilets and bathrooms in the Starfighter.

'You think we can get a hundred thousand gallons

from a pool into this thing? You've got to be crazy. You should have taken a sample right at the start.'

'Oh sure, first thing you do is test for illegal substances in swimming-pools. That's genius. Like dope carriers always dump the stuff there. What they do then? Wait till the water evaporates? Jesus, we've got some real geniuses round here.'

They reported back to the office in Atlanta.

'We've been given the run-around. Either Sol was sucker bait and someone else was running the stuff or those Poles were selling foot powder. What's Washington say?'

'Says you've screwed up.'

'That fucker Campito was a fucking decoy,' said Palowski as they left the office. 'Had to be. Just let me get my hands on the bastard I'll castrate the swine.'

'Too late,' said Murphy. 'They've found his body in the Everglades – or the bits of it the alligators left.'

As the DEA team pulled out of Wilma, Wally Immelmann lay in the Coronary Unit staring bleakly at the ceiling and cursing the day he'd ever got married to that fat bitch Joanie or allowed her to bring her goddam niece over with those terrible girls. They had ruined his marriage and his reputation with that damned recording and he wouldn't be able to show his face in Wilma again. Not that he cared too much about his marriage – at times he was grateful to the little bitches for wrecking it. Infinitely more infuriating were the business consequences of their obscene emails.

Immelmann Enterprises had lost virtually every customer he had cultivated over the past fifteen years and several of them were threatening him with lawsuits. He had tried to contact his lawyers only to be told that they no longer wished to represent a man who was mad enough to send messages calling them 'cocksuckers' and 'motherfuckers', not to mention announcing to the world in the crudest terms and at one thousand decibels that he made a habit of sodomising his wife. Even Congressman Herb Reich had been a recipient of one of the more abusive emails. To cap it all Maybelle's statement to Sheriff Stallard hadn't helped either. The news that the most prominent businessman in Wilma regularly had sex with black employees had spread all over the country and almost certainly was known right across the State. In short, he was a ruined man. He'd have to leave town and change his name and hole up somewhere he wasn't known. And it was all that fucking Joanie's fault. He should never have married the bitch.

In her cell in yet another police station in yet another town Ruth Rottecombe felt the same way about her marriage to the late Shadow Minister for Social Enhancement. She should have known he was just the sort of idiot to get himself murdered at a time when she needed his support and influence most desperately. After all, that was what she had married him for, and she had cultivated that drunken swine Battleby to ensure that Harold's seat in Parliament remained absolutely secure. She tried frantically to make sense out of the chaotic series of events that had led up to his disappearance, but the noises coming from a drunk who alternated whining pleas to be let out of the cell next to hers with vomiting, and on the other side what sounded like a foul-mouthed psychotic on some extremely powerful hallucinogenic drug, made anything approaching rational thought impossible. So was getting any sleep. Every half-hour the cell door was opened, the light turned on and a sinister female detective asked her insistently if she was all right.

'No, I'm fucking not,' she had squawked at her time and time again. 'Haven't you got anything better to do than turn the light on and come in and ask that damn-fool question?'

Each time the detective had said she was just making sure she hadn't committed suicide and she had finally left the light on all the time. After three such sleepless nights Ruth Rottecombe was almost prepared to confess she had murdered Harold. Instead she refused to answer any more questions.

'I did not, repeat not, murder Harold. I didn't harm him in any way at all. I have no idea who did, either. And that's my last word.'

'All right, we'll talk about something we know you did do,' the senior detective said. 'We have proof that you drove to Ipford New Estate with a man in the back of your Volvo estate and dumped him there. We also have proof that he had been in your garage and had been bleeding. You know all that so—'

'I've told you I won't answer any more questions!' Ruth shouted hoarsely.

'I'm not asking any. I'm telling you what is undeniable evidence.'

'Oh, God, why can't you stop? I know all that and it is deniable.'

'Right, but what you don't know is that we have a witness who saw you drag the man out of the back of your car and dump him in the road. A very reliable witness indeed.' He paused to let this sink into Ruth Rottecombe's weary mind before going on. 'What we now need to know is why – if, as you've said repeatedly, you don't have any idea what he had done to land up lying unconscious and bleeding in your garage – you drove him down to that New Estate.'

Ruth began to cry. This time she wasn't faking the tears. 'Harold found him there when he came back from London. At least he said he had. He was out of his mind and tried to pin the blame on me. He was shouting and raving and said I'd picked the man up to have sex with him. I thought he was going to kill me.'

'Go on. Give us the rest.'

'He made me go out to the garage and look at the bloody man. I'd never seen him in my life. I swear I hadn't.'

'What happened then?'

'The telephone rang and it was some bloody newspaper said they wanted to interview Harold about bringing young men to the house, you know, rent-boys.'

For another hour they went on with the questions and got nowhere. In the end they left her sobbing in the Interrogation Room with her head on the table, and went into another office.

'Could be true except for one thing,' said the senior Scotland Yard man. 'That bit of cloth from this fellow Wilt's jeans found in the garage and the fact that they discovered those jeans in the lane behind the Manor House two days after the fire and they hadn't been there when they searched the area the first time. Second, he wasn't wearing any when he was picked up in Ipford. On top of that all his gear, the boots, socks and knapsack, were in the attic of the Rottecombe house.'

'You think she planted the jeans there?'

'I'm damned sure someone did.'

'Christ, what a case. And London's demanding a quick arrest,' said the Superintendent.

They were interrupted by a Woman Sergeant. 'She's passed out or is pretending to have,' she told them. 'We've put her back in the cell.'

The CID man picked up the phone and called Ipford. When he put it down again he shook his head. 'They've moved the bloke Wilt to a mental hospital for what they call "assessment", whatever that means. I suppose to see if he's a psychopath.' He paused and considered the possibilities. There didn't seem to be many rational ones.

One of the other detectives took up the theme. 'Whoever set this little lot up had to be damned abnormal. And this bloke Wilt has been in some weird trouble before. Could be he was paid to torch the house.'

The senior CID man gave the matter some thought. 'I suppose it's just possible but this Inspector Flint doesn't think so. Reckons the man Wilt's too bloody incompetent. Wouldn't know how to set fire to a pile of newspapers soaked in petrol, he's that impractical. In any case, if he'd come to set fire to the house he wouldn't have left such an obvious trail staying at bed and breakfasts and giving his real name. No, there has to be someone else. What beats me is that he and that damned Shadow Minister had head wounds. The Shadow Minister's dead and this other fellow might well have been if they hadn't found him in the road when they did. No, I reckon this Rottecombe cow knows more than she's letting on. I don't care if she has passed out. I'm going to break her. She knows more than she's telling. In any case her background stinks. False birth certificate, high-class prostitute who dupes an MP into marrying her, and on top of that she goes in for sado-masochism with that drunken paedophile swine, Battleby. And of course he's tried to shift the blame on to her. Says she deliberately encouraged him to become an alcoholic so she could control him. I wouldn't be surprised if there wasn't an element of truth there.'

And so the questioning went on and got nowhere.

35

At the Methuen Mental Hospital the female psychiatrist assigned to assessing Wilt's psychological state was having as much difficulty. Wilt had passed all the standard visual and symbolic tests with such surprising ease that the psychiatrist could have sworn he'd spent considerable time practising doing them. His verbal skills were even more disconcerting. Only his attitude to sex remained suspicious. It appeared that he found copulation boring and exhausting, not to say ludicrous and fairly repulsive. His admiration for the procreative habits of earthworms and amoebas who simply reproduced by dividing themselves, voluntarily in the case of amoebas and, as far as Wilt knew, involuntarily by earthworms when they were cut in half by a spade, seemed to indicate a severely depressed libido. Since the lady shrink was completely ignorant on the subject of amoebas and earthworms but keen on what little sex her looks attracted, this information came as a nasty revelation to her.

'Are you saying you would rather bisect yourself than sleep with your wife?' she asked, hoping to draw the inference that Wilt had a tendency towards a split personality.

'Of course not,' Wilt replied indignantly. 'Mind you,

when you meet my wife you'll understand why I might be.'

'Your wife does not attract you physically?'

'I did not say that and in any case, I can't see what that has to do with you.'

'I am merely trying to help you,' said the psychiatrist.

Wilt looked at her sceptically. 'Really? I thought I had been brought here for assessment, not for prurient inquiries into my sex life.'

'Your sexual attitude forms part of the assessment process. We want to get a rounded picture of your mental condition.'

'My mental condition has not been affected by being mugged, left unconscious and beaten over the head. I am not a criminal and by this time I should have thought you'd have recognised that I have all my wits about me. Having realised that, I suggest you mind your own business about my married life. And if you think I am some sort of pervert, let me tell you that my wife and I have produced four daughters or, to put it absolutely correctly, my wife Eva had quadruplets fourteen years ago. I hope that satisfies you that I am a normal heterosexual and a father to boot. Now if you want to make me do some more absurdly simple mental tests, I will happily oblige. What I don't intend to do is discuss my marital sex life any further. You can do that with Eva. I think I can hear her voice now. How clever of her to come to my side at such an opportune moment. Now, if you'll excuse me, I think I'll get police protection.'

Leaving the shrink open-mouthed and gaping through her spectacles he hurried from the room and moved down the passage away from the sound of Eva demanding to see her darling Henry. In the background the quads could be heard telling someone who didn't like what he was confronted with that he wasn't seeing double. 'We aren't twins, we're quadruplets,' they sang in unison.

Wilt hurried on, trying to find a door that wasn't locked and failing. At that moment Inspector Flint emerged from his refuge in the Visitors' Toilet, Eva barged out of the Waiting Room and the psychiatrist left her office and peered short-sightedly to see what on earth was happening and collided with Eva. In the mêlée that followed, the psychiatrist, who had been bowled over and was helped to her feet by the Inspector, revised her opinion of Wilt.

If the formidable woman who had knocked her down was Mrs Wilt – and the presence of the four almost identical teenage girls seemed to indicate that she must be – she could fully understand his lack of interest in marital sex. And his need for police protection. She groped around for her glasses, perched them on her nose and retreated to her office. Eva and Inspector Flint followed; Eva to apologise and Flint more reluctantly to find out how Wilt's assessment had gone.

The psychiatrist looked at Eva doubtfully and decided not to object to her presence. 'You want to know my opinion of the patient?' she asked.

The Inspector nodded. In Eva's company the less said the soonest mended seemed entirely appropriate.

'He seems to be perfectly normal. I did all the routine tests we apply in these cases and I should say he has no symptoms of abnormality. There is absolutely no reason why he should not return home.'

She closed the file and stood up.

'I told you so. There's nothing wrong with him. You heard her,' Eva said sharply to Flint. 'You've got no right to hold him any longer. I'm going to take him home.'

'I really think we should continue this conversation in private,' said the Inspector.

'Don't mind me. I just happen to work here and this is my office,' said the psychiatrist, obviously anxious to get this formidably dangerous woman who knocked people over out of the place. 'You can go and continue your discussion in the Visitors' Room.'

Flint followed Eva out into the passage and into the Waiting Room.

'Well?' Eva said as the Inspector shut the door. 'I want to know what's been going on, bringing Henry to an awful place like this.'

'Mrs Wilt, if you'll just sit down, I'll do my best to explain,' he said.

Eva sat down. 'You'd better,' she snapped.

Flint tried to think how to put the situation to her as reasonably as possible. He didn't want her to go berserk. 'I had Mr Wilt brought here for simple assessment to get him out of the hospital before two Americans from the US Embassy arrived to question him about something that happened in the States. Something to do with drugs.

I don't know what it was and I don't want to know. More importantly he's suspected of being somehow involved in the murder of a Shadow Minister, a man called Rottecombe, and . . . Yes, I know he couldn't murder—' he began but Eva was on her feet. 'Are you mad?' she yelled. 'My Henry wouldn't hurt a fly. He's gentle and kind and he doesn't know anyone in Government.'

Inspector Flint tried to calm her down. 'I know that, Mrs Wilt, believe me I do, but Scotland Yard have evidence he was in the district when the Shadow Minister disappeared and they want to question him.'

For once in her life Eva resorted to logic. 'And how many thousands of other people were around wherever it was?'

'Herefordshire,' said the Inspector involuntarily.

Eva's eyes bulged in her head and her face turned purple. 'Herefordshire? Herefordshire? You're crazy. He doesn't know anyone in Herefordshire. He's never been there. We always go to the Lake District for our summer holidays.'

Flint raised the palms of his hands in submission. Wilt's inconsequential answers were evidently infectious. 'I'm sure you do,' he muttered. 'I don't doubt it for a moment. All I'm saying—'

'Is that Henry is wanted by Scotland Yard for the murder of a Shadow Minister. And you call that all?'

'I didn't say he was wanted by Scotland Yard for murder. They just want him to help them with their inquiries.'

Tom Sharpe

'And we all know what that means, don't we just.'

The Inspector struggled to get some sense into the tirade. And as ever with the Wilts he failed.

In the central concourse of the mental hospital Wilt, who had spent half an hour searching for a way out, had failed too. All the doors were locked and, dressed as he was, he had been accosted by four genuinely insane patients two of whom protested they weren't depressives and didn't intend to have electric shock therapy again. Another two sidled up to him clearly under the influence of some very strong anti-psychotic medication and giggled rather alarmingly.

Wilt hurried on, unnerved by these encounters and by the atmosphere, and cursing the peculiar way he was dressed. Through a window he could see an area of lawn with patients wandering about or sitting on benches in the sun and beyond them a high wire fence. If he could only find his way out there he'd feel a lot better. But before he could make his way into the open air, Eva shot out of the Waiting Room and hurried towards him.

'We're going home, Henry. Now come along. I'm not listening to any more nonsense from that dreadful Inspector,' she ordered. For once Wilt was in no mood to argue. He'd had quite enough of the dim distracted figures around him and the oppressive atmosphere of the mental hospital. He followed her through the main door and towards their car which was parked outside on the gravel, but before they reached it a series of screams echoed through the building.

'What on earth is going on?' Eva demanded of a small and evidently demented man who was scurrying past, panic-stricken.

'There's a girl in there with breasts that move from one side to the other like the clappers!' he yelled as he ran past.

Eva knew who that girl was. With a silent curse she turned and pushed her way into the hospital through the crush of patients trying to escape the awful sight of scurrying bosoms. Emmeline's rat Freddy, encouraged by the effect it was having and at the same time alarmed by the shrieks, was up to its old tricks with a vigour it had never shown before. The sight of a third pubescent breast apparently changing from right to left and back again at a rate of knots was too much even for heavily sedated mental patients. They had been faintly aware that they were not at all well but this was altogether too much. Hallucinations couldn't come any worse than this.

By the time Eva reached Emmeline the rat was hidden in her jeans. As mad hysteria broke out in the concourse and spread through the entire hospital and even into the Secure Area, Eva, dragging Emmeline and the other three girls, who were enjoying the chaos Freddy's imitation of a rampaging breast had caused, forced her way through the deluded mass struggling in the doorway and, thanks to her size and strength, out into the open air. By the time they reached the car Wilt was already inside it and cowering in the back seat.

'Get in and cover your father,' Eva ordered. 'We mustn't let him be seen by the guard on the gate.'

The next moment Wilt was on the floor and the four girls were kneeling on top of him. As Eva started the car and drove down the drive she glanced in the rear-view mirror and glimpsed a dishevelled Inspector Flint hurtle out of the door of the hospital, trip and land face down on the gravel. Eva put her foot on the accelerator and five minutes later they were through the gates and heading for Oakhurst Avenue.

36

Inspector Flint arrived in his office in a state of confusion. His conversation with Eva had confirmed him in his belief that whatever mess Henry Wilt had got himself into he was not responsible for the death of Harold Rottecombe. Tripping on the gravel and then being trampled over by a herd of maddened lunatics had given him fresh insight into Wilt's inconsequential view of life. Things just happened to people for no good reason and, while Flint had previously believed that every effect had to have a rational cause, he now realised that the purely accidental was the norm. In short, nothing made sense. The world was as mad as the inmates of the hospital he had just left.

In an effort to regain something approaching equanimity he ordered Sergeant Yates to bring him the notes on the Rottecombe murder case he'd received from the Chief Superintendent who had been cross-examining Ruth the Ruthless. Flint read them through and came to the conclusion that, far from being involved in the death of the Shadow Minister for Social Enhancement, Wilt had himself been the victim of an assault. Everything pointed to the Shadow Minister's wife. Wilt's blood in the garage and in the Volvo, the fact that she was seen in

Ipford New Estate and caught on the motorway camera in the middle of the night, and in Flint's opinion that she had been on sado-masochistic terms with the paedophile 'Bobby Beat Me' Battleby whose house had been torched. In addition there was a motive. Wilt had been in the lane behind Meldrum Manor. His jeans had been found there two days after the fire but they hadn't been there when the police had searched the lane on the day after the fire. It followed that they had been put there in order to implicate him in the arson. Finally and most damning of all his knapsack, socks and boots had been recovered from the attic in Leyline Lodge and he was hardly likely to have put them there himself. No, everything pointed to Mrs Rottecombe. Wilt had no reason to kill her husband and if the Shadow Minister suspected or, worse still, knew his wife had connived in the fire, she had every reason to want him dead. At this point Flint spotted a flaw. Wilt hadn't been found dead. He'd certainly been assaulted by some young thugs on the New Estate and the Rottecombe bitch had brought him there without his jeans or walking boots. Why had they been removed? That was the mystery. He went back to the theory that she'd needed them to indicate that he'd been involved in the arson of the Manor. But why leave them in the lane two days later than the fire? That only deepened the mystery. The Inspector gave up.

In Hereford Police Station the Chief Superintendent, urged on by Downing Street, hadn't. He no longer believed Wilt had had anything to do with the torching of Meldrum Manor or the death of the Shadow Minister. He had ordered the police at Oston to find witnesses to Wilt's journey and to trace his route as far as they could. 'You know where he stayed each night,' he told the Inspector there. 'What I want now is for your men to check where he bought his lunch and get as clear an idea as you can where his walk took him and where it ended and when.'

'You talk as if I have an army of constables here,' the Inspector protested. 'I have precisely seven, and two are extras brought in from the next county. Why don't you charge this man Wilt?'

'Because he was the victim of an assault, not the perpetrator of one. And I don't mean he was just mugged in Ipford. He was bleeding from a head wound when he was in the Leyline Lodge garage and when she drove him down to Ipford. He's not on the suspect list any more.'

'So what does it matter where he went?'

'Because he may have been a witness to the fire and who started it. Why else did this woman take him down there? In any case, he has amnesia. Can't remember who or what hit him. That's the official psychiatric report.'

'What a hell of a case,' said the Inspector. 'I'm dashed if I understand it.'

Which was exactly what could be said for Ruth the Ruthless. Deprived of sleep, endlessly cross-examined and made to drink extremely strong coffee, she was desperate and unable to give any coherent answers to the questions being put to her. To make matters worse she had been charged with hindering the course of justice, falsifying a birth certificate and, thanks to Battleby's seriously damaging allegations, purchasing the paedophile magazines he revelled in. The two so-called journalists Butch Cassidy and the Flashgun Kid had had writs issued in relation to the attacks by Wilfred and Pickles and the media were having a field-day smearing her in the tabloids. Even the broadsheet papers were using her reputation to attack the Opposition.

At 45 Oakhurst Avenue Wilt was having something of a hard time too, convincing Eva that he didn't know where his walking tour had taken him.

'You didn't want to know where you were going? You mean you've forgotten?' she said.

Wilt sighed. 'Yes,' he said. It was easier to lie than to try to explain.

'And you told me you had to work for a course next term on Communism and Castro,' Eva persisted. 'I suppose you've forgotten that too.'

'No, I haven't.'

'So you took those awful books with you?'

Wilt looked miserably at the books on the shelf and had to admit he'd left them behind. 'I only meant to be away a fortnight.'

'I don't believe you.'

Wilt's sigh was audible this time. It would be impossible to explain his wish to see the English countryside without any literary associations to her. Eva would never understand and almost certainly would suppose there was another woman involved. 'Suppose' was too mild a word: she'd be certain. Wilt went on to the offensive.

'What brought you back so quickly from Wilma? I thought you were going to be over there for six weeks?' he asked.

Eva hesitated. In her own way she was suffering from self-induced amnesia about the events in Wilma and in any case, coming home to learn her Henry had been mugged and was in hospital and incapable of recognising her had been so traumatic, she hadn't had a spare second to consider what had caused Uncle Wally to have an infarct and Auntie Joan to turn so nasty and throw her and the quads out of the house. The only answer she could come up with was that their return had been necessitated by Wally Immelmann's two heart attacks.

'Couldn't have happened to a better bloke,' said Wilt. 'Mind you, the way he swilled vodka with his steak at the Tavern in the Park and followed it up with that murderous drink he called A Bed of Nails, I'm surprised he's lived so long.'

And with the happy thought that the ghastly Wally was finally getting his comeuppance he went to his study and made a long and uncomplimentary entry about Mr Immelmann in his diary. He hoped it would be the bastard's obituary.

37

In the two separate bedrooms which they occupied at 45 Oakhurst Avenue the quads were each compiling dossiers for Miss Sprockett which, had he seen them, would definitely have finished Uncle Wally off. Josephine was concentrating on his sexual relations with Maybelle with emphasis on 'forced unnatural acts'; Penelope, who had a natural gift for mathematics and statistics, was listing the vastly different rates of pay between whites and blacks at Immelmann Enterprises and other industries in Wilma; Samantha was comparing execution numbers in various states and Wally's expressed preference for public hangings and floggings to be mandatorily shown on prime-time television instead of less inhumane methods; and finally Emmeline was describing his collection of weapons and their use in language that was calculated to horrify the teachers at the Convent, in particular Wally's description of flame-throwers and 'barbecuing Nips'. All in all they were ensuring that the havoc they had caused in Wilma itself would be compounded by the justified disgust their dossiers would provoke among the parents of the girls at the Convent and their friends in Ipford.

*

Down at the police station Inspector Flint was enjoying himself too, berating Hodge and the two men from the US Embassy.

'Brilliant,' he said. 'You come in with Hodge here and refuse to identify yourselves clearly or explain why you've come and expect me to kowtow to you. And now you're back to tell me there's not a shred of evidence of any drugs in this man Immelmann's place. Well, let me tell you, this isn't the Gulf and I'm not an Iraqi.' By the time he'd finished working off his feelings he was in a good humour. The Americans weren't but there was nothing they could say. They left and Flint could hear them calling him an arrogant Brit and, best of all, blaming Hodge for misleading them. He went down to the canteen and had a coffee. For the first time he appreciated Wilt's view of the world. Ruth Rottecombe still maintained, in spite of the pressure brought to bear on her, that she had no idea who, if anyone, had murdered her husband, and the Scotland Yard detectives were at long last beginning to believe her. Harold Rottecombe's shoe and the sock with the hole in it had been found, the shoe wedged in the stream and the sock on the ground in the field. Much as they wanted a conviction, they were forced to admit that his death might well have been purely accidental.

Wilt's account of getting drunk on whisky in the wood had been substantiated by the discovery of an empty bottle of Famous Grouse with his fingerprints on it under a tree. His route had been worked out by the police in

Oston; there had been a thunderstorm and everything fitted his account exactly. All that remained was to uncover the person who had set fire to the Manor House but that was proving impossible too. Bert Addle had burnt his boots and the clothes he had been wearing, and had washed and scrubbed the pick-up he had borrowed. The friend who owned it and who had been in Ibiza on holiday at the time had no idea it had been used in his absence.

In short, everything added to the mystery. The police had questioned everyone in Meldrum Slocum who had been connected with the Manor and the Battleby family in the hope that they would know of anyone who was in league with 'Beat Me Bobby' to torch the place for him. But Battleby was so thoroughly disliked as a boorish drunk that nothing came of that line of questioning. Had anyone a sufficient grudge against the man? Mrs Meadows nervously admitted that he had sacked her but Mr and Mrs Sawlie were adamant they were with her when the fire started and for an hour before she had been in the pub. Above all the Filipino maid was a major suspect because of the pressurised cans of Oriental Splendour and Rose Blossom which had contributed so explosively to the conflagration, but she had the perfect alibi: it had been her day off and she had spent it applying to become a trainee nurse in Hereford. She hadn't got back to Meldrum Slocum until the following morning because the train had broken down.

Reading the report, Flint could find nothing to explain

the arson or the possible murder of the Shadow Minister. The confusion would never be unravelled. For the first time in his long career as a policeman he began to appreciate Henry Wilt's refusal to see things in terms of good and evil or black and white. There were grey areas in between and the world was dominated by them to a far greater extent than he had ever imagined. It was a revelation to the Inspector and a liberating one. Outside, the sun shone brightly down. Flint got up and went out into that sunshine and walked cheerfully across the park.

In the summer-house in the back garden at Oakhurst Avenue Wilt sat contentedly, stroking Tibby the tail-less cat happy in the knowledge that this was his own version of Old England and that he would always remain a suburban man. Adventures were for the adventurous and he had strayed from his proper role in life as husband to Eva with her multitude of temporary enthusiasms, and as the father of four uncontrollable girls. He would never again venture from the routine of the Tech, his chats over pints of bitter with Peter Braintree at the Duck and Dragon, and Eva's complaints that he drank too much and had no ambition. Next year they would go to the Lake District for their summer holiday.

Wilt

Tom Sharpe

'This delightful book . . . lives, rises and triumphs
by a slicing wit'
Daily Mirror

'Superb farce . . . If you don't laugh your head off,
Crippen wasn't guilty'
Tribune

'Mr Sharpe's face has a gritty satirical edge to it, and the world
his embattled central character inhabits is all too real'
Sunday Times

'Tom Sharpe piles slapstick upon slapstick with the ingenious
dexterity of a music-hall illusionist'
Sunday Telegraph

'The funniest detective story in years'
Evening News

arrow books

Vintage Stuff

Tom Sharpe

'When Tom Sharpe turns his attention to a very minor public school
. . . the result is predictably savage. Hoaxes, chases, car crashes,
shootings, and general mayhem. Wicked riotous humour'
Daily Telegraph

'Wildly hilarious pot-shots at the public school system and the
sacred cows of adventure fiction'
Observer

'You'll enjoy this wild and, in places, wildly funny story . . . It is an
hilarious send up of the Dornford Yates style of thriller with some
modernistic Sharpe barbs added'
Daily Express

'Britain's leading practitioner of black humour'
Punch

arrow books